CHELSEA CURTO

To Mike, who has his own sun tattoo. You keep my days bright. I'm glad we got pancakes. Thanks for being my forever Valentine.

CONTENT WARNINGS

This is intended to be a fun novella, but it does have a few parts of deep discussion. Within these pages you will find:

-Multiple EXPLICIT open-door scenes with on-page sexual content. It is graphic and detailed. If that isn't your jam, proceed with extreme caution.

-Brief discussion of divorce and the mention of infidelity (no on-page scenes or detailed descriptions)

-Brief discussion of IVF and infertility (no on-page scenes or detailed descriptions)

-Brief discussion of self-consciousness relating to one's body

-Explicit language

As always, my DMs are open if you want to chat further. Take care of yourselves, friends. You are loved.

ONE
MAGGIE

"I HAVE A PROPOSAL FOR YOU." My best friend and photographer extraordinaire, Jeremiah, doesn't use a proper greeting when I answer his phone call in the middle of my work day, taking a rare moment to catch a breather in the hospital break room. With over two decades of friendship under our belts, the formalities are nonexistent. "Let me finish explaining before you say no."

"If you know what my answer is going to be, why bother asking?" I prop my phone in the crook of my neck and pour a steaming cup of coffee. A single inhale, and I'm rejuvenated, fresh life in my legs after back-to-back surgeries. An ache is forming between my eyebrows, and I use my thumb and forefinger to rub the pain away.

"When I had the idea in the shower last night, your name popped into my head. I couldn't stop thinking about you."

"I'm flattered, but it'll never work between us. We like the same things."

"Dicks and gin and tonics." He laughs and the chuckle warms my soul.

"Please tell me you didn't kill someone and that's why you're calling from Stockholm Fashion Week. Working with bodies and watching every *Law and Order: SVU* episode doesn't make me equipped to bury one," I say. "I wouldn't be a good fit. I'm sorry. It's not you, it's me."

"Your conscience doesn't allow you to keep a library book for longer than the allotted hold time. Do you honestly think I'd come to you if I needed to cover up a murder?"

"Fair point. Okay, if it's not an ethical dilemma, what is it?"

"Did you see the post I shared on my Instagram story?"

"No." I take a sip of the caffeine, savoring the bitterness of the unsweetened beverage. "I've been in the OR all day."

"It's a photo shoot with two strangers. They don't meet until the day of the session."

"Sounds interesting."

"I want to do one. It'll be the start of a new series. When I get home, I need a break from all the content I've been working on lately. High fashion portraits and runway walks are amazing, don't get me wrong, but I want to mix it up."

"That's great, Jer. Your work is so versatile. Adding another component to your portfolio is smart."

"I had this idea for a Valentine's Day-centered shoot after seeing another photographer do an intimate session with strangers. All consensual, of course. It was a *hit*, Mags. The internet loved it. For mine, I'm thinking we'll do flower petals on the floor. Candy hearts scattered across a picnic blanket. We'll also lean into the sexy side of not knowing the other person. Maybe we can do some tasteful boudoir photos to showcase that formed intimacy. It wouldn't be provocative, of course. Just enough to create tension the audience craves. I'll keep it laid-back and fun."

"And you thought all this up in the shower? Impressive."

"Yeah. Which leads me to you. You're my pick for leading lady, of course. My muse. What do you think?"

I'm silent as I process his words. My mug hovers halfway to my mouth, and a drop of forgotten coffee spills on the floor.

"Let me make sure I'm understanding this correctly," I start. I must be hearing him wrong. Maybe I'm suffering from brain fog, and delusion is confusing my auditory receptors. "You're saying you want me to do a sexy photo shoot with someone I don't know? In lingerie I don't own? While eating candy hearts that say 'LOL' on them?"

"No." Jeremiah pauses, considers. "Okay, yes, when you put it that way, it's exactly what I'm saying."

I can't help it. I burst out laughing. It's full-on hysteria slanting through the air. I wipe tears from my eyes, the salty tracks staining my cheeks.

"Oh my god," I say through another round of giggles. "The more you talk, the more absurd it sounds. I'm sure the world wants to see my pasty white ass and the extra pounds I've been carrying around since Christmas."

"Mags," Jeremiah interjects. "I know it's not something you'd normally do."

"It's not something I'd ever do," I correct him. "This might be a groundbreaking question, but why not hire someone who knows what they're doing?"

"Because I don't want professionals," Jeremiah huffs. "Society sees plenty of edited images on billboards and in magazines of people who look nothing like the average man or woman. Why stand up and preach about embracing our bodies and differences if we don't show them on a public stage? The core focus of the shoot is real humans and how they aren't perfect. It's about chemistry and the dynamic between two individuals, leaning into the uncomfortable and creating a story. I'm going to send you a link so you can look at an example, okay?"

"What if there isn't any chemistry? What if we show up to do these sexy, intimate photos and there's no heat?"

"Then we call it a day and move on with our lives."

I stare at my coffee, the dark swirls offering me no advice. "Can I think about it?"

"Of course you can. I'll be back in town next Wednesday. Want to grab dinner with Lacey and give me an answer?"

"Sure. If I say yes to the shoot, what day do you have planned?"

"A week from Saturday. Are you free?"

"On actual Valentine's Day? Oh my god, Jer. That's so cliché."

"After the shoot, I'll buy you dinner. We can get drunk and laugh about what a good time you had."

"That doesn't sound like a bribe at all."

"Would it help if I told you I've vetted the guy and he seems like a catch?"

"I'll take that into consideration, but don't get too excited."

"Love you, Mags."

As soon as I hang up, my phone buzzes with a message from him. I open the link and am directed to a website featuring the type of photos he must be envisioning. I scroll through the page, mesmerized.

Damn him.

Jeremiah was right.

A story is unfolding on my screen, and it looks *fun.* The couple in the shoot is positioned away from each other in the first images, wearing pinched smiles and exhibiting awkward body language. They're tense, the distance between them—literally and figuratively—is unmistakable. The deeper down the page I go, a shift happens. It's noticeable, an obvious change in the dynamic. The snapshots show a natural progression, like the metamorphosis of an actual couple and the stages of their relationship.

Soon, they're laughing, rigidity relaxing into familiarity. His gaze lingers on the corner of her mouth in a black and white portrait. Her teeth sink into her bottom lip as she watches him talk with his hands. The tension, palpable even through a digital image, is *hot*.

Another scroll down, and the scene changes again. There's less clothing. The woman, a curvy girl wearing a navy blue bra and underwear set, is positioned on the man's lap. A bulge is visible through the unzipped jeans that sit low on his hips. Curls of hair peek out from the waistband of his boxer briefs. He presses a kiss to the column of her throat, staring at her like she hung the moon. Her head tilts back, hands gripping his shoulders like her life depends on it.

Heat inundates my face. The session is hardly the most raunchy thing I've seen. I watch porn. I read filthy romance books with every kink known to man. Still, it's as if I'm interrupting a private, sensual moment between a *real* couple intimately acquainted with the other's body, mind, and soul, no part undiscovered.

I click my phone closed and fan myself, the warmth yet to subside.

When was the last time anyone looked at me that way? Stars in their eyes, hands frantically clawing for me, not a care in the damn world about what's happening around them? A tornado could come by and they wouldn't realize it, too enamored with the sight in front of them.

Years, probably.

Maybe a decade or more.

Maybe never, if we're being honest, and that's really fucking *sad*.

A thousand thoughts sweep through the turntables of my mind. Jeremiah is an established and well-liked photographer. He has over a million social media followers, and his posts garner thousands of likes and comments. He's collaborated with some of the most prolific figures in the modeling industry and is damn good at his job, possessing a true talent for finding beauty in the small moments, the mundane ones others often overlook.

Not Jeremiah, though.

He captures those milliseconds before they become a distant memory, immortalized through the lenses of his expensive Canon and the vintage Polaroid he purchased back in high school; the still-functioning camera is the first he ever bought. A shoot like this is unfamiliar territory for him, but I know he'd knock it out of the park in the way he does everything else: with purpose and intent, resulting in stunning works of art. It's a high honor he wants me to help, to be an integral part of this project he's excited about.

Shit.

I know myself. I'm going to say yes to the photo shoot. Maybe this will be good for me. It'll break up the monotony of my personal life, which lacks any substance. I go to work, I come home, and I repeat the boring cycle.

After a nasty divorce three years ago, I've sworn off relationships and dating, vehemently avoiding men at all costs. The celibacy is self-imposed, preferring the use of my vibrator over the mess another heartbreak would bring. The photo shoot isn't a date by any means. It's a moral obligation to help a friend. Besides, it's not like the guy and I would hit it off and fall in love.

That kind of fairy tale only happens in romance novels. If I've learned anything over the years, it's that my life mirrors a tragedy rather than a comedy, not a single happily ever after in sight.

TWO

AIDEN

"YOU'RE GOING TO HATE ME." My best friend, Shawn, smirks from across the table.

His arm is draped over the back of the chair beside him, a colorful tattoo sleeve on full display. Ink spirals down the ridges of his biceps, and his muscles nearly rip the shirt he's wearing.

Showoff.

"I already hate you," I reply. I take a sip of my beer, alcohol a necessity to combat the headache forming across my temples from the loud, pulsing music of the club he's dragged me to. "I'm out past eight p.m. This shit sucks. I want my bed."

"You'll want it even more in a few minutes."

I raise my eyebrows, and for the first time since I walked into this overcrowded building, bodies pushed together and the smell of sweat and spilled drinks permeating the air, I'm nervous.

Shawn and I have been friends for years, stretching back to the days where we lined up beside each other at Pop Warner football in elementary school. Our companionship spans decades, consisting of divorces, children, and contract deals with the NFL. He's the youngest head coach in league history, and was recently named Sexiest Athlete Alive, an accolade I tease him about mercilessly.

He thrives in the spotlight, gravitating toward people like a moth to a flame. The more social he can be, the more conversations he can have, the more galas and fundraisers he can attend: the better. His phone is constantly lighting up with messages from family, friends, or his players seeking advice and words of wisdom. Everyone who comes in contact with Shawn Holmes loves him; a vitalizing beacon of positivity.

For me? This club is a place of fucking nightmares. I hate crowds and loud gatherings. My job as a pediatric oncologist is stressful as hell, and the last thing I want to do at the end of a fourteen-hour shift is go to happy hour or meet up with a group of friends to shoot the shit late into the night. That was reserved for my twenties. At forty-five, I'm just fucking *tired*.

Shawn texted me earlier and said we needed to talk, though, and I agreed to accompany him to Hell on Earth if he promised to buy drinks. A futile proposition, since he's recognized everywhere he goes, women—and men—flocking to him. We've had three complimentary rounds sent over so far tonight, all from various interested parties trying to gain his attention. I don't care who he goes home with. I'm just glad I don't have to foot the bill.

"What did you do?" I knock back the last sip of my beer.

"I volunteered you for something," he answers. His confidence has slipped a bit, and I see him fidget with the collar of his shirt. It looks like he could have bought it for ten bucks at Walmart, but I'm certain it cost at least two hundred from some designer I've never heard of.

"Okay. Like, a fundraiser? I'll check my calendar and–"

"A photo shoot," he interrupts.

I blink. My brain is turning murkier by the minute, and clear, rational thoughts are becoming increasingly difficult with every bottle I down. There's no way I heard him correctly. "Can you repeat that, because I think you just told me you put my hand up to stand in front of a camera and model?"

"Do you know Jeremiah Porter?"

"Who the hell is that?"

"He's a local photographer. He shot my *GQ* cover last month, and we got to talking. Nice guy. I told him to stay in touch about upcoming projects, and he called me a couple days ago with this idea for a new shoot."

"And you heard that and thought I would be interested? Your friend with no social media who doesn't know how to take a selfie?"

"The angle he's going for is real people," Shawn continues. He sits forward in his chair and stares at me. "People who work nine-to-five jobs, have some flaws, and don't look like what you'd see on television. When he explained his vision, I thought you would be perfect."

I blink again. This has to be a joke. Some elaborate ploy to pull my leg, because no way in *hell* am I posing in front of a camera. "You're out of your mind."

"I haven't gotten to the best part yet." His lips split into a grin. It's the smile that makes panties drop and women go weak in the knees. I want to swat the stupid elation off his face. He's lucky I'm teetering toward inebriation, otherwise I would be storming out of here and not bothering to look back to hear the rest of this lunacy.

"I can't wait to hear how this gets better."

"You don't meet the woman until the day of the shoot."

Yeah, I must be shit-faced. The only reaction I have is laughter. I keel over, clutching my side as I howl. Beer almost comes out of my nose, and I think I've reached a level of insanity I never thought achievable. "You're right," I say. "It gets way better. Taking photos with a stranger I've never met. Surrounded by other people I don't know.

Where my picture will end up on the internet. No, thank you."

"What if I told you she's pretty?"

"I don't care if she's Anne fucking Hathaway. It doesn't change my mind. The answer is no. Let me know if I need to spell it out for you."

"Anne Hathaway is your celebrity crush? Really? I pegged you as a Scarlett Johansson guy."

If looks could kill, Shawn would be six feet under, and I'd have no remorse. "No way. I'm not doing it. Sorry, your friend is going to have to find someone else."

"Aiden." He sighs, sounding exasperated, like I've done nothing but annoy him for thirty-eight years. "Since Katie left, your life is stagnant and boring. You don't do anything. You work, and you go home."

"I prefer it that way."

"Aren't you lonely?"

"Nope."

Not really. Not in the way Shawn assumes. I don't want a relationship. I'm too busy with work and my kid, shuttling her to swim practice and keeping up with her social calendar. Throw in trying to juggle my own sanity, and there's zero time left for dating. People think my occupation is altruistic at first. They hear the big buzz words: Cancer. Doctor. Kids. There's this gasp of surprise. Adjectives like *selfless* and *important* are lobbed my way as if I can change the world. The positivity is short-lived, lasting only until I keep my phone silent all day, messages going unanswered because I'm busy and don't have time to talk about my favorite food or ideal date via text. Women lose interest pretty quickly after that, and thus I begin another round of being alone.

Some sort of female presence would be nice, though. I love my kid dearly, more than anything in the world. But another adult in the picture, even if just for a few hours, has been a craving of mine as of late.

A night or two of physical release and intelligent conversation not revolving around pep rallies or homecoming dresses. Hands other than my own sliding under the waistband of my joggers, gripping my dick. My cum landing somewhere other than on my stomach... like down a woman's throat. Her on top of me, thighs bracketing mine as she rides me to oblivion. Spending all day in bed, sheets rumpled and dirtied as I eat her out under the light of the rising sun.

Fuck.

Too many beers. Not enough action.

"It's not a date," Shawn continues. "It's a few hours of social interaction. Look, Aiden. It would be good for you to do something unconventional for once. I think you will have a good time. You and the woman have a lot in common, so you wouldn't feel like giving yourself a lobotomy when you talk to her."

"What?" I snort. "Is she also a doctor who prefers staying home over going out with friends who volunteer her for stuff?" Shawn grins at me again, a silent confirmation, and the air whooshes out of my lungs in a shaky exhale. "Oh, shit."

"She's a doctor. Pretty. Wicked smart. Jeremiah thinks you two will get along great."

I nod at the passing server for another drink. *Fuck*, this next beer won't be enough. I need something stronger. Like a cleaver to my skull or a whole handle of vodka. Hearing Shawn call her pretty stirs up something dark inside me, a tornado of acidity. Is it jealousy that he's seen her first? Disappointment that she's probably already talked to him and fallen in love like every other woman who comes by?

"This is important to you?" I ask. It must be. He wouldn't have signed me up for something he knows I'd hate for shits and giggles.

"Yeah. Jeremiah came to me asking for help. You know I'm a big advocate for small businesses. Sure, he's established in the industry, but this particular project is special to him. He's been nothing but kind to me in the times we've spent together, and I thought I could pay some of that kindness forward."

"Okay." The guilt trip works, tugging pathetically at my heartstrings. "I'll do it. But you owe me big time."

"Trust me, Aiden." Shawn's smile is back in place. He reaches over and clasps me on the shoulder. "I think after all of this is said and done, you'll be the one thanking me."

THREE
MAGGIE

"THIS LO MEIN IS BETTER than any orgasm I've had." Lacey, one of my other best friends, groans around the bite she's inhaling. The outburst is punctuated with a loud slurp. The man two tables over looks up from his menu, intrigued, and she winks at him. "I could bathe in this sauce and die happy."

Lacey and I met in med school, sitting beside each other in microbiology and dissolving into an unprofessional fit of giggles when the professor said *orgasm* instead of *organism*. I'm surprised we weren't thrown out of the class. Often loud, always enthusiastic, she has no quiet mode, exuding an enviable zest for life and sexual escapades.

"What would you like us to do with your drawer of sex toys?" I down a spoonful of hot and sour soup with the question, the liquid burning my tongue.

Lacey, Jeremiah, and I are situated around a high top at our favorite Chinese restaurant in the city. It's busy for a weeknight, the room bustling with hungry patrons. Casual conversations flow freely over marinated duck and Kung Pao chicken.

We're three days out from the photo shoot, and I told Jer I'd give him my answer over dinner. Deep in my heart, I knew I'd always say yes to helping him, personal concerns about feeling out-of-place aside. He'd never set me up for failure or embarrassment, and if he can see this vision vividly, I'm going to hold on to the faith that soon I will, too.

"Imagine if you died while using a vibrator," he says. "How would you explain it to your family and friends? Would you want some fake cause of death listed in your obituary? Or the truth?"

I consider the question over my last bite of food. "The truth, because what a way to go. The headline could read: 'She died while doing what she loved most... taking care of herself.'"

"'Woman accomplishes what no man is capable of: a mind-blowing orgasm,'" Lace adds.

"'She was a vibrant woman.'"

"'She came, and she went.'"

"If you two keep the innuendos up, that man is going to proposition you both to spend the night with him," Jeremiah says.

"Wouldn't be my first time," Lacey quips. She takes a sip of her wine, an alcohol-induced blush creeping up her neck. "Mags, how are you feeling?"

"About a threesome? I'm not drunk enough to consider it."

"About the photo shoot," she clarifies. "But good to know where you stand on the other topic."

I pick up the mug of green tea I've been sipping steadily through the evening. The tannins stick to the inside of the porcelain as I swirl the drink around. It takes a second for me to speak, and neither of the pair hurries me along.

"I'm going to do it," I say, hesitant excitement lacing my words. Jeremiah squeals, and Lacey pumps her fist in the air. "Why the hell not? It's about time I put myself back out there after the divorce. It's not a date. There's no pressure. It's two adults taking photos. That's it."

"It'll be way more fun than what you'd find on a dating app anyway," Jeremiah says. The reassurance helps, and the knot of tension residing between my shoulders loosens. "This could be a test run before the real thing, when you actually *are* ready to get back out there."

"The dating apps aren't all terrible," Lacey counters. A strong rebuttal is turning the wheels in her head. "I've used them and had outstanding success."

"Yes, to sit on someone's face. Not to actually get to *know* them," Jer tosses back.

"I *know* what patterns I prefer their tongue to work in. What else is there to learn?"

"That's the thing," I say, interrupting their crass sidebar. "I don't want to date again."

"Ever?" they ask in unison.

"Not for the foreseeable future. Life is fine as it is. I'm happy. Work is going well. Why should I try and undoubtedly mess it up by involving a man?"

"Well. The guy you'll be working with seems great," Jer says brightly.

"I know you know everyone, but how did you meet him?" I ask.

"I haven't met him yet. His name is Aiden Wood, and he's best friends with Shawn Holmes, the dreamy football coach I've shot a couple of times." When Lacey and I stare at him blankly, he rolls his eyes. "Tattoos. Biceps for days. Athletic body with massive hands. And, if the rumors are true, an impressive dick he knows how to use *very* well."

"Ah." I nod. "Chivalry isn't dead. It's merely disguised as impressively sized dicks."

"I was tipsy last night and accidentally—okay, I purposely went down a Facebook rabbit hole, winding up on one of Aiden's sisters' profiles." There's a gleam in his eyes, a conspiring glimmer proudly boasting he's in possession of precious information and won't give it up easily. "I am very excited about Saturday."

"Is that all you're going to share? His name?"

"Yup. I'd hate to ruin the surprise. It'll be worth the wait."

I grumble a string of expletives under my breath and cross my right leg over my left. He's being elusive, and I hate the secrecy.

"Why Valentine's Day?" Lacey asks. "It's the worst holiday in the world."

"Amen to that," I agree. "Look around. There's love-sick couples everywhere. Half of them will end up divorced. Another quarter will grow to resent each other and stick the marriage out despite being woefully unhappy. Shouldn't we be sharing our love for our significant others year-round, and not just on a commercialized day designed to spike retail sales?"

"All good points," Jeremiah says. "But, Mags, you're a biased participant. You can't, in good faith, speak on the day."

He's right. I resent February 14th. It hasn't always been this way. I used to love the holiday. There would be a bouquet waiting for me in the kitchen when I woke up, complete with a hand-written love note. There would be candy and chocolate-covered strawberries on the bedside table. A nice dinner at a fancy restaurant with an expensive bottle of wine.

Four years ago, it was the day Parker, my ex-husband, told me he wanted a divorce. I came home from work and found a stack of papers waiting for me on the dining room table. Three hundred and sixty-five days later, on the very same day, my marriage officially ended. There was no discussion. No fighting. There was no pleading or problem solving. It was just... the end.

In hindsight, he wasn't right for me. I know that now, but I'd been wearing rose-tinted glasses at the time. We met at a fundraiser. He was donating a lot of money. I was representing my former hospital. I backed into him, spilling a glass of wine on his leather shoes that cost more than my rent. He apologized profusely for being in my way. And the rest, as they say, is history. One night forever changing the course of my life.

We dated for two years and had all the deep conversations a couple in love should have. Discussions on politics and children. Finances and goals for the future. Real estate preferences and familial backgrounds. We aligned perfectly in our beliefs, and I knew I had found The One.

After our wedding, the pressure to have a family started. His parents sent us small baby gifts in the mail. A rattle here. A pacifier there. The message was clear: Put your career on hold and pop out a child. That's all I was to them; a breeding machine. It didn't matter how hard I'd worked at becoming an accomplished neurosurgeon. If I wasn't a mother, I hadn't succeeded.

Parker and I tried. We tried, and we tried, and we tried. Nothing worked. IVF treatments didn't work. Acupuncture didn't work. After extensive tests and lab work, we found out I was infertile, through no fault of my own. Just another mystery of life, and I drew the short straw.

Grappling with the discovery was difficult. We went to couples counseling, and I started individual therapy. I threw out other options: Adoption. Surrogacy. My confidence was throttled. Intimacy became nonexistent. Every time Parker looked at me, I saw the disappointment and resentment in his eyes. I was a failure, and nothing I ever did in life would make up for my shortcomings.

I don't miss the person who never looked at me like he was a starving man and I was his key to survival. I don't miss the woman I turned into, the lack of compliments and affection building a mountain of self-loathing. Therapy has been a godsend. I've compartmentalized the past. I've grieved it and made peace with it. Parker wasn't my person, and even if the nights get lonely, they're infinitely better than being with someone who isn't head over heels in love with me.

This photo shoot could kick off a new era. An appreciation for the day and reclaiming it for reasons other than relationship torment. Maybe I'll buy myself flowers and a new piece of lingerie. I'll enjoy a glass of chardonnay in a steamy bubble bath as I get myself off after a fun day with a guy I'll never see again.

I'll imagine this mystery man—*Aiden*—running his hand up my leg. Nudging my knees apart and trailing hot, searing kisses down my neck as he slides a finger inside me, stretching and filling me beyond belief. He'd be game for anything I want to try, offering a resounding agreement when I propose a new position or the addition of a toy.

"Mags? Daydreaming over there?"

I crash back to reality. My eyes adjust to my surroundings as I realize I'm not in the privacy of my home but with my best friends, one of whom is grinning at me like she can read my mind.

"Sorry. Distracted." I fumble for my water glass, the liquid refreshing down my parched throat. The room feels hotter than when we sat down, and it takes three long sips until my equilibrium balances out. "Thank you for convincing me to do the shoot. This is going to be a good thing."

Jeremiah beams. "Wait until you see his smile."

FOUR
AIDEN

"YOU LOOK like you're struggling to take a shit."

I glance up from the mound of clothes littering my bed to find Maven, my foul-mouthed sixteen-year-old daughter, leaning against the door jamb of my room. She's still in her one-piece bathing suit from swim practice and holding a sports drink full of electrolytes. A puddle of water pools on the hardwood floor beneath her, and I wave my security deposit goodbye with every chlorinated drop.

"Want to try that again without the colorful commentary?" I ask. I'm not mad about the vernacular; if *shit* is the worst thing to come out of her mouth, I deserve a pat on the back for a parenting job well done.

She laughs and joins me at the footboard to assess the war zone she's walked into. "Are you going on a trip? Cleaning out your closet? Please tell me you're donating that god-awful pair of loafers. Or, better yet, tossing them in the incinerator. Good riddance."

"Glad to see your bluntness hasn't faded with age. I'm being subjected to something against my will, thanks to the idiocy of Uncle Shawn."

"Is he really an idiot if he won an award from the NFL for his contributions to his community, dedication to preserving local ecosystems, and global involvement not just in sports, but advocacy for humankind?"

"How much did that prick pay you to flaunt his achievements?"

"Fifty bucks," she says, taking a sip of her drink. "What's going on?"

"I'm doing a photo shoot tomorrow. Your uncle," I say bitterly, "signed me up for the gig. It's with a stranger, too, and I'm out of sorts about it."

"Whoa. You're leaving the house?"

"I leave the house plenty."

"Not for something other than the hospital."

"I take you to—"

"Or swim practice."

"Okay, I also—"

"Picking me up from Mom's doesn't count, either."

My mouth snaps closed. The little weasel has backed me into a corner. *Checkmate.* "Fine," I relent. "You might have a point."

"I can't believe you're going to model. That's so fun."

"We have very different definitions of fun."

"Why do you look so stressed out?"

"Besides the fear of having to do something I'm not going to be good at with a woman I don't know in front of professionals?"

"Dad." Mae gives me a look. I'm a sucker for those puppy dog eyes, and she knows it. I sigh and rub my temples. "Spill."

"Promise you won't make fun of me?"

"I'll only make fun of you if you wear a pair of jorts out in public."

"What are—never mind. You know I don't buy into religious

stuff, and I'm not sure what higher power or god might be out there. It sounds stupid, but it feels like the universe is telling me I *have* to do this shoot. As much as I'm dragging my feet, my gut says it's important. A pivotal moment in my life I can't miss out on. I've only experienced a sensation like this one other time, and I think I'd be stupid to ignore it."

"And when was that?"

"When I met your mother."

Maven's eyes widen in surprise.

In these moments of quiet contemplation and consideration, my daughter looks so much like me. Her face is a mirror image of my own, down to the slope of her nose and the line of her jaw. Hazel eyes that show every glimmer of emotion, cursedly readable, and matching forehead wrinkles when we're thinking too hard.

The other components of what make her unique—her stature, mannerisms and lack of filter—come from Katie, my ex-wife. The woman I fell in love with in a large, loud lecture hall, the smell of freshly sharpened pencils and dry-erase markers hanging in the air. We met in Trigonometry. I was in the class because of a screwup with my high school transcripts. She was there because, for a fleeting moment, she aspired to be a math teacher. I made a terrible joke about tangents and co-signs. She burst out laughing. My cheeks turned red, and we were married at twenty-three.

Our family looks different now from a half decade ago when we would spend weekends at museums and weeknights gathered around the table for a communal dinner. We're no longer whole, broken into autonomous parts after an amicable divorce and Katie's remarriage, but Maven's still my greatest gift. Even when she's giving me shit and ribbing me, a constant amusement for her, there's an indescribable proudness in knowing she's *mine*. As a parent, there's no greater joy than looking at your offspring and seeing the love and devotion you've instilled in them reflected tenfold.

"Anyway," I continue and gesture at the clothing. I've emptied every drawer from my dresser and yanked every shirt off its hanger. "That's enough philosophy for one night. What looks best?"

"You're *not* wearing a Ramones T-shirt in pictures that are going to end up on the internet," Maven says, horrified. She shoves me out of the way. The faded cotton top with a hole in the armpit gets tossed on my nightstand, covering the lampshade and darkening the room.

"I love that shirt."

"It's uncool." Another item of clothing—a black V-neck this time—is next to be sacrificed. "Don't you sleep in this? Come on, Dad. I swear if you tell me you own a pair of white New Balances, I'm going to stay at Mom's for a week."

I bark out a laugh at her fierce mockery. "I don't *sleep* in it. It's casual wear. Keep making fun of the guy who pays your allowance, and see where it gets you."

"Your best friend is a literal millionaire and he buys me stuff all the time." Mae taps her cheek, deep in thought. She points at the gray sweater I've been considering for the better part of an hour. It matches the clouds on a snowy day, or a dull nickel found on the sidewalk. Heads up, of course, a rush of good luck awarded to its discoverer.

I need all the fucking luck I can get.

"That one. It'll bring out your eyes." Her chin lifts toward a pair of jeans next. They're fairly new, never worn and impossibly stiff. "Those, too."

"Shoes?"

"Black boots and your nice jacket."

I exhale a grateful sigh and pull her into a tight hug. "Thanks, kiddo. I'm going to ignore the paid labor and pretend you helped out of the kindness of your heart."

"I did. I promise. Love you, Dad." Mae grins. "So this photo shoot is with a woman, hm?"

"Oh, Christ. Not this again."

I know exactly where this conversation is headed. Maven is a self-proclaimed romantic, and I have the 2005 film adaptation of *Pride and Prejudice* to thank for her affinity with love stories. The movie has become an obsession, and she constantly asks if there's anyone *new* or *special* in my life. When a woman looks my way at a swim meet, honing in on my button up and tie, Maven concocts a narrative in her head, saying maybe *that one* is my soulmate.

I don't have the heart to tell her I think soulmates are a load of shit. The idea that there's another person out there made specifically for me? I'm cynical. A surefire nonbeliever, and I'm not buying into it.

"Do you know who she is?"

"Nope."

"What if you two meet, hit it off, and fall in love?"

"Not happening. It's not a date. It's a business transaction on behalf of someone else."

"No wonder you're single. You refer to women as a business transaction."

"I mean, I'm not looking at this as a romantic encounter. I'm doing it to help a friend."

"If she's nice, do you promise to ask her out for coffee?"

"Sure," I answer flippantly. It gets her off my back, even if it makes me a shitty father for lying.

Maven claps. "Yes! Progress. First stop, espressos and croissants. Next stop, walking down the aisle."

"Keep dreaming, kid," I say.

It's not like I'm going to meet this woman and fall in love with her. It's impossible, a stupid thought to even consider.

Still, though, that persistent hum of importance continues to cackle through me, a deafening roar I can't tune out.

FIVE
MAGGIE

MY TEETH CHATTER as the frigid air plagues my lungs. I lift my chin and take in the 10,000 square foot warehouse Jeremiah owns. The industrial building looms in front of me, an ominous stretch of construction appearing less inviting and more intimidating the longer I stand outside, delaying the inevitable.

With a final deep breath of courage, I pull open the glass door and walk inside with my head held high. A gust of heat envelops me, a warm, welcomed hug helping to quell the jitters racking my body. My shoulders become pliant, relaxing and loosening away from my ears to their natural resting position.

"You can do this, Maggie. It's a couple of photos. You'll be home by dinner. No big deal," I whisper to myself. A glance at the modern clock on the wall tells me I'm ten minutes early, barely considered on time by Jeremiah's stringent standards. Assistants are already hard at work. Someone is fixing a floral arrangement, trading out a rose for a daisy in a pink vase. Another is fluffing white pillows on an aquamarine couch, organizing the squares into a perfect line.

"There's my star!" Jeremiah's voice filters across the room.

I wave and walk toward him. The gray floor of poured

concrete is the only dark component of the space, a stark juxta-position to the walls swathed in various colors and patterns. Pink stripes, green rectangles, purple stars and white hearts wink at me as I pass.

A high ceiling stretches above me, a whopping twenty feet up. Skylights illuminate the drab path I shuffle across in ethe-real hues of yellow and orange. I look around, seeing dozens of props set up. A bed, complete with a headboard and footboard, covered in a navy duvet. A clawfoot tub, a dance floor, and a spinning disco ball. In the corner, the back left section of the room, is a parked lime green Hyundai.

"Hey." I greet Jeremiah with an embrace. I hold on longer than necessary, reveling in the silent support he's sending me, conveyed with a tight hug around my shoulders and a kiss to the top of my head.

"Holy shit." He releases me and lets out a long whistle. "Those jeans look incredible on you. Spin." He twirls his finger and I do a small circle in place. "You have a figure, Mags, and it's hot as hell."

I blush at the compliment. The clothing was a frenzied purchase, bought on impulse yesterday afternoon. The denim highlights my curves, hugging my thighs and accentuating my hips and backside. When I looked in the mirror before I left, I felt *good,* liking who I saw staring back at me.

"Thanks."

"Aiden is close," Jeremiah continues. "When he gets here, I'm going to do a rundown on the itinerary with you all, then send you to hair and makeup. After that, we'll get started."

I look over my shoulder at the entrance in anticipation. A spool of eagerness unravels through me.

Aiden Wood.

I laid in bed last night and stared at the ceiling, wondering what he might look like. Is he tall? Does he have dark hair or light? Is his skin tan, sun-kissed and tawny from hours spent outside? Or is it more of an olive complexion? What about glasses? Tattoos? Facial hair?

As if on cue, like I've summoned him to materialize and conjured his presence from my curiosity, the door to the warehouse swings open. Sunbeams glint in through the entryway behind a figure moving swiftly inside. The man—obvious from the posture—is only a shadow. A whisper of unknown until the barrier closes and I can finally, *finally* see him properly.

My vision blurs, solid figures turning to indistinguishable colors and shapes. Time stops, and the world narrows down to a singular entity: him.

I blink, and the formidable haze settles to pristine clarity so I can soak him in.

He's not very tall. If we were to stand side by side, there might be an inch or two of height difference between us, and the advantage would go to me. His coiffed hair is auburn, slightly wavy on the top of his head while cut close to his ears. Near his temples are strands of gray, salt and pepper mingling with the brown. A neatly trimmed beard covers his cheeks and hides his jawline. Draped over a corded forearm is a large coat, and the gray sweater he's wearing is rolled to his elbows, teasing me with inches of bare skin.

He's wildly attractive. It's not Hollywood handsomeness that would have throngs of women flocking to him, nor is it the blatant sex appeal of a rugged hero from a romance novel. It's more subtle and delicate, brought alive by small details and the way he carries himself. One hand in his pocket and his shoulders rolled back. A confident stroll as he walks toward us. The flick of his gaze to my face, then my legs, and back up again, approval etched in the corner of his mouth like granite and finely cut stone.

"Aiden. So glad you could make it," Jeremiah says.

27

Aiden's lips, full and pink, twitch marginally and curl into a small smile. His hazel eyes crinkle, nearly sparkling under the fluorescent lighting. "Jeremiah. It's so nice to meet you."

His voice is deep, a baritone timbre that makes my thighs quake. Commanding, while also as smooth as melted chocolate. My face flushes, heat gliding down my back as I relish in his perfect enunciation.

"You too." Jeremiah nudges me, his elbow landing in my ribs. I take that as my cue to speak.

"Hi," I say. My voice wobbles and I clear my throat. "I'm Maggie Houston."

"Hi, Maggie Houston. I'm Aiden Wood." He ends his introduction with a full smile, and I think I melt.

His hand withdraws from his pocket and extends my way. I accept it, and his fingers lace around mine, vines clinging to a tree to survive. The pad of his thumb presses into the pulse point of my wrist, applying the slightest bit of pressure.

The touch is innocent, yet it seems significant. Some monumental blip in history happening in a warehouse outside the city center as snow falls from the sky. I stare at where we're joined, unable to let go. I'm not sure I want to. Aiden doesn't release me from his hold or pull away, either. I think we've fused ourselves together, a cement casing binding us.

A loud clank and a litany of curse words ends our interlude. I see one of Jeremiah's assistants wrestling with a large light near a bench, a woman with curly hair the perpetrator for the unwanted interruption in our private moment. Aiden's grip tightens, a cursory attempt to hold on for just a little longer, before he steps away and abruptly severs our contact. I'm cold without him, a desolate chill settling over the spot where his warm hand just was.

"Oh," Jeremiah says cheerfully. "This is going to be fun."

SIX

MAGGIE

"BEFORE WE START," Jeremiah continues, "I want to talk about today. There's no pressure to perform in a certain way. I want you to do what feels comfortable. If something doesn't feel right, I want you to say no. If you want to stop at any point, either of you, please tell me, and we'll call it quits. Sound good?"

Aiden turns to me. He's distracting, a presence that's impossible to ignore. Broad shoulders. Contemplative eyes staring with vigorous intensity. A set of wrinkles between his brows I want to wipe clean, rubbing out the divots with my thumb and smoothing over the unmarred skin.

He's quiet as his head tips to the side, a conversation passing between us. We don't need to speak; I understand the gesture with shocking ease. It's an invitation to create a unified front, tackling today in tandem.

I dip my chin in affirmation, and his eyes sparkle again, a luminescent swirl of brown and green. "Sounds great, Jer," I say. "We'll do our best to deliver."

"Take a few minutes to get to know each other, then we'll get rolling." With a wave, Jeremiah disappears.

A pleasant silence settles, a quiet calm broken by the scuff of

Aiden's boot on the floor. He runs his hand through his hair. A few strands jostle free from their perfectly layered position, sweeping across his forehead in a field of waves. The gray I noticed earlier runs deeper than previously suspected. It's starting to infiltrate the rest of his scalp, a sexy silver tone buried under the lighter shade.

My gaze bounces to his hands, scouring any visible landscape to study him more deeply. There's a mole on his left pointer finger, and a jagged scar runs along the ridges of his knuckles. He leans forward on the balls of his feet, the position drawing him an inch nearer. I can smell his cologne, a mix of woodsy spice and fresh citrus. The scent surges up my nostrils and I inhale deeply, committing the smell to memory.

"Are you—"

"How do you—"

We speak simultaneously, tripping over each other in a race to get the questions out. I bite my lip to keep from giggling. Aiden blushes, the apples of his cheeks turning pink.

"Sorry," he apologizes. He makes a wild gesture with his hands in my direction, a combination of circles and points. "You go first. Please."

The reins of power are in my possession with the singular word. I'm the captain, in charge of the direction of our conversation. I can't help but wonder how that *please*, the kind, polite *please*, would sound whispered in my ear. Traversing down my neck and across my chest, a lover's caress. A subtle shake of my head disperses the thoughts.

I pause before asking my question, sidestepping out of the way of a large stand with three lights attached to the top. I smile politely at the assistant who apologizes for nearly dropping the contraption on our toes before she expeditiously departs, leaving us alone again.

"Are you nervous?" I settle on. It's the simple route to take, a segue into a casual exchange without diving into personal details. Maybe we'll get there later, when the brick walls I've constructed start to crumble, and the tension of the unknown dissolves.

Aiden relaxes. The faint frown lines around the corners of his mouth soften. He stands straighter. Still a smidge shorter than me, I notice, even at his full height. He's probably five foot eight inches on a good day.

I wonder if it bothers him.

It certainly doesn't bother me.

"Nervous? I'm petrified. My friend, Shawn, is the one who volunteered me. Didn't tell me until I was three beers deep and couldn't tackle him for his stupidity. What the hell am I supposed to do with my hands? Do I have a good side or bad side I don't know about?"

A brick slides out with his sincere answer, the fortress around my heart becoming less protected, more prone to weakness and devastation. "That makes two of us. Jeremiah can be very convincing," I say. "It's both a blessing and a curse."

"You two are close?"

"We met in high school, and we've been best friends since. He's wickedly talented, and a good person to have in your corner."

"I could hear his passion behind this project. It's important to love what you do. You're a good friend for helping him out."

"Do you think we're going to have to take our clothes off?" I blurt out. I close my eyes and smack my forehead with the heel of my palm, wishing the ground would swallow me up. "Shit. Sorry, that was weird as hell. Let's pretend I didn't ask that out loud. How embarrassing."

Aiden grins. The smile is slightly lopsided, lifting higher on the right side of his mouth than the left. And, I realize seconds later, it's one of the most beautiful things I've ever seen. He smiles with his whole being, a bright explosion of color and giddiness working across his face. There's teeth and eye wrinkles. A scrunched nose and the drop of his head backward as his shoulders shake.

"Sorry." He chuckles. "I'm not going to be able to forget that. Though if we're being honest, for my sake, I hope we are going to take them off." His gaze roams down my figure in an assessment that's far from cordial. I squirm under the slow drag of his pupils, noticing how they linger on my hips the longest.

"Why's that?" I ask. It's raspy. My throat is parched and my lungs are seizing, in desperate need of oxygen. All the air has been sucked out of the room, nothing but extinguished embers from a kindled fire left behind.

"You're a beautiful woman, Maggie. I'd be an idiot to hope for anything else."

The hair on my arms stands up. My blood hums. My heart stutters and lurches, latching onto the blunt words protectively, hoping I can keep them forever. I can tell it's not a generic line used on other women. It's authentic, tailored just to me.

"Mags. Aiden. Hair and makeup time. Let's go," Jeremiah barks out from across the room. Another moment disrupted and I rub the back of my neck. I'm usually not one to ignore my surroundings, but I'm completely distracted.

Aiden blanches, glee fading to horror. "Why does he sound like an asshole?"

"Because he runs a tight ship. The second those lights turn on and he has a camera in his hands, it's like I've never met the guy I took to senior prom. We can stop whenever we want, but until we reach that point, be prepared. He's ruthless. What Jer says, goes."

"What did we get ourselves into?"

"Hell," I say brightly. "Want to hear the bright side?"

"Please."

That wretched word again.

"We don't have to suffer alone. We're in this together."

"I like the sound of that," he says. It's husky and lower than before. Rich, with a promise behind the words. A tone I'd like to hear again, outside these walls and somewhere private, maybe. With a parting glance, Aiden turns on his heel and heads toward Jeremiah.

Oh, shit.

I am in a heap of trouble.

SEVEN

AIDEN

MAGGIE HOUSTON IS RADIANT. I struggled to get words out when her gaze locked on mine. My mind went slack, riddled with uselessness. Nothing I could say felt adequate enough. We're on two different levels; she's in the stratosphere, on a pedestal of loveliness, while I reside on Earth, a mortal who will never be good enough.

Even with blush on her cheeks, lipstick painting her mouth a shade of pink, and her previously straight hair turning to slight waves after seeing the stylists, there's an easy, natural beauty about her. The glow is similar to a summer day when the air is warm, and the sun is bright in the cloud-free sky. You tip your head back, close your eyes, and relish in the blissfulness of serenity, a picture of perfection.

That is what it's like to be in her presence.

It's overwhelming.

Her long hair is a mixture of blonde and brown streaks, the shade of caramel or honey. Her eyes twinkle like finely cut green emeralds, tangoing with excitement. The smile on her lips is gregarious and wide, but also sultry and tempting, capable of bringing the world to its knees in worship. On her left cheek is a single dimple, sharply carved into the smooth, blemish-free skin.

Her sinister figure is reminiscent of sculptures I've seen in museums, the ones I've always found attractive, cut out of marble with soft curves and hips and thighs. She's all woman. And her ass? It's so round, so goddamn *perfect*, it has me wondering if my heart is going to flatline. Deceased by Maggie Houston's backside, and in need of resuscitation.

My favorite part about her isn't the way her jeans hug the swell of her bottom or the dip in her shirt hinting at hidden cleavage. It isn't the way her tongue sneaks out of her mouth to wet her lips between sentences, or how she smiles at almost everything.

It's how tall she is. She stands inches above me, easily. Some men are embarrassed they're not six-foot-something, willing to sell their soul for a more "masculine" stature and shying away from partners who tower over them.

Me?

I don't give two shits. I've always gravitated toward women who have the height advantage, finding the slope of their legs, the length of their calves and thighs as I run my hand up a never-ending stretch of skin stupidly sexy. And when they're wearing heels, or, in Maggie's case, wedges?

I'm a fucking goner.

I wonder how they would feel wrapped around my waist, the block of leather pressing into my lower back with sharp precision. The scrape of straps trailing down my spine as she adjusts her position on a bed, guiding me and asking for *more*.

I'm trying not to stare, not to gawk at her like some creep, but it's impossible not to be curious about her. Which means I dutifully trail behind her to the wooden bench made of deep mahogany where Jeremiah is waiting for us. We stop short of the furniture, and Maggie tenses beside me. Her shoulders square back in a defensive stance. The corner of her mouth drops, the smile melting to a subtle frown.

"Together, right?" I murmur in her ear. Her hair tickles my cheek as she peers at me with wide eyes.

"Together," she repeats. Inadvertently, as though in a fit of nervousness, her hand slips into mine. It takes a beat before she registers what she's doing, and when she does, she starts to pull away. I squeeze her palm, keeping her joined to me, letting her know I'm a man of my word. She's not in this alone.

"You can stay, Maggie." *Fuck*, her name is like an exaltation from angels. It rolls off my tongue, the same way it would if I whispered it into her neck or chest in a moment of passion. "Do you want to come up with a phrase or word we can say if one of us needs a second to pause?"

She exhales and nods. Her fingers drum against the back of my hand, a string of twine linking us together. "Good idea. What about 'picnic'? It looks like that's what we'll be doing after this first scene."

A blanket is set up on a patch of fake grass to the right of the bench. A wicker basket and a vase of wildflowers sit on the ground. Boxes of candy hearts, the same ones I attached to all the Valentine's Day cards Maven gave out to her classroom back in elementary school, are scattered across the pink and white plaid.

"Nice choice." My thumb rubs across the plane of her knuckles, an instinct to comfort taking over. "Want to play a game to keep today interesting?"

She drops our hands and turns to me, chest grazing my shoulder. The glide of the fabric of her shirt against mine is a shock to my system, jolting me awake. It's stronger than holding her hand or the whole damn cup of coffee I chugged on the way here, an injection of heat to my veins.

"What kind of game?" Maggie asks. She arches her eyebrow

and folds her arms across her chest. I deserve a gold fucking medal for not staring at her breasts, the movement lifting them higher. "Tread lightly, Aiden, because I don't want to feel Jeremiah's wrath."

My dick twitches. My name spills from her mouth effortlessly, making it seem like she's spoken it a million times before.

Fucking hell. That's really fucking nice.

It would sound even better if she screamed it, I bet.

"Twenty questions?" I suggest, firmly snapping the lid closed on *Provocative Sounds Maggie Houston Might Make.* "Nothing perverse. Mundane stuff. Favorite foods. Pet peeves."

"I'm down," she says. "Only if I can ask you first."

"Deal."

"Okay," Jeremiah says. "We're going to start with you all talking on the bench. I prefer my photos to be more candid, less posed. I'm going to be clicking while you two socialize. Do what feels natural, and ignore me."

Maggie and I take a seat on the weathered wood. There's a heart carved into it, just above the armrest, with a pair of initials in the middle. It's faded over time from sunlight, and the letters are barely visible.

I wonder if those two are still together.

Two souls, forever tied.

To my right, Maggie angles her body toward me. Her hands fold into her lap and she lifts her chin. She keeps her feet planted on the ground, and I notice her toenails are painted a ruby red.

"I guess this makes us friends," she says.

"Do all your friendships start on a bench while having your photo taken?"

"Yeah. Yours don't?"

I chuckle at her humor and shake my head. "I'm more of a couch or bean bag fan myself."

"Laidback, I see. What's your favorite food?"

"Pickles."

"Of all the food in the world, you pick a jarred vegetable?"

"They're technically fruits," I say. "I read it on a Snapple cap once."

She laughs, and a gleam brightens her eyes. "I didn't think I would be learning anything today, but you proved me wrong."

"Happy to be of service. Time to educate me. Tell me your favorite food."

"Meatballs. I have six siblings, and my parents worked a lot when I was younger. They made huge batches of pasta and meatballs for dinner. We'd eat it two, three nights a week. Even today, it's my comfort food."

This isn't as painful as I thought it would be. I'm not dragging my feet, begrudgingly complying with instructions. I'm genuinely interested to hear what Maggie has to say, eager to learn more. Testing the waters, I scoot closer to her. As I do, I smell ripe oranges. It's intoxicating. Fresh. Sweet.

When I subtly inhale and try to savor the scent, I realize I'm totally and completely fucked.

EIGHT
AIDEN

"IT'S YOUR TURN FOR A QUESTION," Maggie says.

Her words snap me out of the lapse I've slipped into, soaking in her proximity. It's been so long since I've been near a woman, I've pathetically entered some sort of trance because of her. I nod and push the sleeves of my sweater farther up my arms. It's warmer than I thought it would be in here, and I wish I had brought something less constricting to wear.

Her eyes drop to the sliver of space near my biceps. She studies my skin, from the patch of moles below my elbow down to my wrist in a slow perusal. I can't help but curl my fingers into a fist. It's showing off, I know, the egotistical portion of my brain flexing the tendons so she can see my muscles. I want her to be aware of what I lack in height, I make up for in other departments. The power to lift her if I wanted to. Onto a counter. A table. Against a wall.

She can take her fucking pick.

Her gaze moves across my shoulders to my face. We hold eye contact and her teeth sink into her bottom lip, canines creating puncture marks in the pink.

Yup.

I'm definitely fucked. I want to sink *my* teeth into her lip and tug her toward me. I want to trace the outline of her mouth with my thumb and find out if she tastes like oranges, too.

"What's your biggest pet peeve?" I ask. It's not the most urgent question floating in my mind, but it's the most appropriate one.

"People who don't return their shopping carts. If you're an able-bodied human, push your cart back to the little cart holder."

"Do we know if there's a scientific name for the cart holder? Should I call them LCH's? Cart garages? Cart parks?"

"It physically pains me that I'm not able to dig out my phone and research this topic thoroughly."

"The lazy cart drivers are my pet peeve, too. Perhaps we can research them together. We'd get through the data faster."

"Yeah," she says. "Perhaps we can."

Her eyes twinkle, and I like this easiness between us. It feels good to have a conversation with someone new, no pressure to say the right thing. It's not a date or work. It's not a parent-teacher conference. There are no responsibilities or expectations. We're just kind of here. We just kind of are. And I'm glad to just *be* with her.

"Okay, it's clear you two don't hate each other," Jeremiah calls out from behind his camera. He motions for an assistant to shift the backdrop to the left a quarter of an inch, nodding when he likes the new position. "Thank goodness. Can you get a little closer for a few more shots?"

Maggie and I move at the same time. Her foot nudges mine, and her body weight becomes unevenly distributed. My knee knocks hers. Her hand lands on my thigh as she steadies herself. Fingers dig into my quadriceps, and her nails drag up my jeans on a tortuous path. There's a vice-like hold on the curve of my leg.

I suck in a sharp inhale at the contact, caught off guard by the position we've found ourselves in.

"Shit," she squeals. Her face flushes a deep crimson. The hand six inches from my dick stays in place, and I'm not mad about it. "Sorry."

"For what?"

"Basically feeling you up."

"Must not be that sorry, because you're still doing it," I joke. I smile after I say it, hoping to defuse the tension. She releases me and scoots across the bench, creating miles of distance between us. "Hey. I was just kidding."

"That was uncalled for. I shouldn't have—"

"Maggie." My tone is laced with a demand that she look at me, a register I've never used before. Her eyes lift to meet mine, unsure. *There she is.* "You can grip my thighs whenever you want. There's enough there for multiple people to latch on to. Haven't been to the gym in weeks. I kind of liked when you touched me, but you should have bought me dinner first. I know I'm irresistible."

"Oh, my god." She reaches out and gently shoves my shoulder. "Are you going to tease me for the rest of the day?"

"Without a doubt. We're friends, right? Teasing comes with the territory."

"You know, in retaliation, maybe I'll tell you what side is your bad side."

"That wouldn't be retaliation. It would be a great help. I'm surprised my face hasn't broken a camera yet." I turn toward Jeremiah. "Sorry if I'm ruining your shots, man."

He doesn't bother to come out from behind the lens, squatting to shoot a photo at an upward angle. I hear another click.

"This is the most fun I've had at work in months. Please, keep it going."

"That's a high compliment," Maggie whispers to me. "He gets to go all over the world."

"Wow. Shooting two amateurs in a warehouse in D.C. is better than New York Fashion Week? Look at us. Who would've thought?"

"My shoulders have finally come down from my ears, I think." She smiles and rolls her neck to the side. "Is this what it's like to be relaxed?"

"I'm not sure I've been relaxed since the late 90s, so I'm not qualified to answer."

"You're qualified to answer my next question."

"Hit me, Houston."

"In two words or less, tell me what you do for work."

"Children. Cancer."

"You're a doctor?" she breathes out.

My heart hammers in my chest, a loud and poignant thing. I'm surprised she can't hear it. "Yeah. An oncologist, specifically. What about you? What do you do?"

"Brains. Surgery." It's barely above a whisper, nearly discernible over the cacophony of other sounds around us. To my ears, though, she's almost shouting.

"Holy shit, Maggie. A neurosurgeon? That's incredible. Here I was thinking I was cool, then you roll up and knock me down five million pegs. And rightfully so."

She pulls at the collar of her shirt, a sleeveless black top that shows off her sculpted shoulders. I follow the track of her hand as she touches the thin fabric and runs her finger down the line of her throat.

"It's not that great," she stresses. "I have lots of help. I'm not doing it on my own. There's no I in team."

My eyebrows furrow together and I cross my arms over my

chest. "You're diminishing your achievements and selling your-self short. Why?"

It's reckless to wonder, teetering out of the *woman I'm bidding adieu to in two hours* zone and into the dangerous area of *woman I'd like to get to know on a more personal level while I fuck her brains out* arena.

"In the past, I've been told to do just that—to diminish my achievements." Maggie smooths her palms over her thighs, moving halfway down the length of her legs. "When you hear something so many times, you start to believe it."

"Whoever told you that can fuck right off. Celebrate that shit. There's less than 4,000 neurosurgeons in the United States, and I'm sitting next to one of them. Hey, everybody." I raise my voice, and all the people on set peer at me. "Can we take a minute to appreciate how smart this woman is? She's a goddamn genius, and she's sitting here talking with me? I'm a lucky bastard."

Approval flickers across the face of the woman Maggie was talking to earlier during hair and make up—her friend, if I had to take a guess. Jeremiah finally shows his face, giving me a grin. A woman off to the side covers her heart with her hand.

"I'm mortified," Maggie says, fighting off laughter.

"But are you proud of yourself? Fuck everyone else in the world. Right now, if I asked you again what you did for work, how would you respond?"

"I'm a neurosurgeon. And I'm damn good at it."

"That's my girl," I murmur, and she goes full scarlet. "Doesn't that sound good?"

"It sounds great. In more ways than one." She holds my gaze for two, three more beats before dropping her eyes to my thighs. She lingers there for a moment then breaks her reverie to smile at Jeremiah. "Ready for the next scene?"

"Let's take ten, everyone, then reconvene for the second setup!" Jeremiah says.

Maggie stands and makes a beeline for her friend. They bow their heads together and speak in hushed tones. I'm unable to move. Still chasing that reckless high, my lip curls up.

She's a fan of praise?

I really *am* a lucky fucking bastard.

NINE

MAGGIE

"I THINK WE HAVE A SITUATION," I say to Lacey. We've tucked ourselves into a private corner, away from the hustle and bustle of the set. I need a second to breathe before we start again.

"What's going on?"

"Aiden. Aiden is the situation. I'm flirting with him. Willingly. And I'm letting him flirt with me, too."

"The audacity." Lacey gasps in fake horror, a hand flying over her mouth. "A single woman flirting with a man? I've never heard of such a scandalous thing in my life. They'll hang you in the town square for public indecency."

"You're the worst." I groan, taking a steadying breath. Three big gulps of air in, three out. The meditation does little to slow the staccato beat of my heart or the ache deep in the caverns of my belly.

A good-looking man is something any woman can appreciate. I marvel at firm lines of masculinity and crooked noses, broken in a sports match or on the playground when they were younger. I roam over the ridges of defined muscles, hours spent in the gym. I melt at wicked smirks and playful winks.

Experiencing a physical reaction to the opposite sex without intimate physical contact, though, is new, and Aiden is the catalyst. My underwear is damp, the lace stained with arousal. Under my shirt, my nipples are hard, pebbled from the feel of his thigh under my palm. My fingers itch to run through his hair and hold onto his shoulders, to feel his skin against mine.

"He's hot, Mags. That much is obvious. He's clearly into you. Why not have some fun and see what happens?" Lacey asks.

"What do you mean?"

"Keep flirting with him. Get to know him. Ask him questions."

"I haven't been this personal with a man in years. And before that, my relationship had been so boring, there was zero chemistry or affection. What if I'm bad at the whole flirting thing?"

"He's a man. We give the bare minimum, and they eat it up. Speaking of, too bad he's not eating *you* up. That would fix all your problems."

Yeah, I think gloomily. *Too bad.*

"Maggie," Jeremiah gushes. He takes the position next to Lacey, beaming at me. "I knew I was right in asking you to do this. There's so much emotion present. A story is unfolding for the lens, which isn't an easy feat. Walls are coming down. I'm so proud of you."

"Thanks, Jer."

My gaze drifts to the middle of the room. Aiden is near the bench we previously occupied. His hair is getting combed by a woman who keeps flashing him smiles. He nods politely to the story she's sharing. As if sensing he's being watched, his eyes unexpectedly meet mine.

Shit.

I expect him to look away, but he doesn't break. A heady surge of need spiderwebs through me. I should look away, but I can't. *He* should look away, but he doesn't. This goes past a prolonged accidental glance. It's purposeful, crafted on the desire of wanting to study all his features, and simply wanting *him*.

Aiden is the first to break, and I don't think it's willingly. He licks his bottom lip and turns his focus back to the oblivious woman. She's unaware someone else is holding his attention, and a surge of smugness settles over me.

His glance was a definite demonstration of possessiveness. It's as if he's staking a claim on me, daring anyone else to snatch me up because I'm undoubtedly his. And...

I like it.

I've never been treated like I'm someone's sole focus. Their highest priority and most sought-after prized possession. I've always craved that feeling of consumption. Aiden Wood, a man I've known exists for a shorter amount of time than it takes me to get to and from work, has loudly and unequivocally made me feel more wanted, more special in fifteen minutes than others have over half a decade.

A flame kindles at the base of my spine as I stare at his profile. The curve of his chin. The length of his neck and throat that lead to collarbones I've never found noteworthy before on a man. On him, though, they're merciless in their pursuit to neutralize my brain, reducing me to an unintelligent mess.

Keep flirting with him.

Okay. I can do that.

I swallow and walk toward him. When Aiden sees me approaching, he offers what I interpret as an insincere apology to the woman he's talking with, a wide smile aimed my way.

"They're called cart corrals, by the way. I looked it up. Didn't want you to lose sleep over it. And, since the internet never lies, we can continue on with our lives knowing the correct terminology," he says.

My heart wants to burst, and more bricks fall. *Cart corrals.*

What a silly thing to be excited about. I don't try to hide my grin, courtesy of his investigative research on my behalf. "How kind of you. Tonight I'll climb into bed and have blissful dreams of a world where everyone puts their carts away."

"My work here is done." Aiden tucks his hands into his pockets and rocks on the balls of his feet. "This isn't too bad, right? I thought it was going to be a lot worse, and I was apprehensive as shit on the Metro ride over. My friend might live to see another day."

I laugh. "Look at you being generous. I think it's definitely bearable."

"Fuck it, we might as well go all in, right?"

"It's too late to turn back now. The pictures can only get better."

"I appreciate your optimism, Maggie, but the day is still young. Plenty of time to derail the progress we've made."

"Speaking of young, I have a question for you."

"Let's hear it," Aiden says.

"How old are you?"

"I'm forty-five. I turn forty-six in July, and knowing I'm closer to fifty than forty is fucking terrifying. What about you?"

"I'm thirty-four. My birthday is in April."

"If I knew anything remotely cool about astrology or moon signs, I'd use them to try and impress you. But I don't, so I'll have to settle on something less interesting. What are some of your hobbies?"

"I love to read and spend time with friends. Jeremiah, who you know, and Lacey." I point to the pair watching us. Aiden waves. "When the weather's nice, I rollerblade to the museums. I like to eat, and go to the occasional sporting event. My favorite holiday is Halloween, and I love decorating. I prefer spending time at home rather than at a bar or club. The older I get, the more I appreciate those quiet moments on the couch. Sorry, I'm rambling."

"Don't apologize. You can tell me whatever you're comfortable with. I'm enjoying learning about you."

"What do you do in your rare free time?" I ask.

"I work a lot, which I'm sure you can commiserate with," he says. "Sports are something I enjoy, too. Watching, obviously. Pretty sure I'd tear a hamstring if I tried to be semi-athletic. I like to read. Thrillers are my favorite, but I'm open to any work of fiction. Speaking of, you didn't say. What's your genre preference?"

"Romance. There's something so gratifying about picking up a book and knowing the two characters you fall in love with on the pages will fall in love with each other, too."

"My daughter loves romance novels. Can't get her to put them down. You'll have to tell me some of your favorite authors. She's always looking for new books to read."

My breath catches in my throat and the world spins to a screeching halt.

"You have a daughter?"

TEN
MAGGIE

"YEAH, I DO," Aiden says. Tension is painted on my face, an obvious accessory as he pulls back. "Oh, shit. Did you think I was—*fuck*. Sorry. That was my fault for casually dropping a bomb on you. I should have started this whole speech with the important information that I'm also divorced. I've been single for years."

"You're divorced?"

"Yeah. Going on five years now."

"Sorry, I don't hate kids. I just thought maybe you were a scumbag, and I was caught off guard."

He laughs, a deep rumble I feel all the way down to my toes. "No, I'm just a dipshit man who got excited to talk to you and said everything out of order. Let me try this again: Hi, Maggie. I'm Aiden. I'm forty-five, divorced, and single. I also have a daughter. Want to be friends?"

"Only if you tell me about your daughter. What's she like?"

A flip switches and Aiden lights up, brighter than the North Star. "Her name is Maven. Or, Mae, as I call her. She's sixteen, a junior in high school, and loves to swim and read. Her favorite subject is English, and she wants to be an editor for a major publishing house when she graduates college."

"Wow, she sounds incredible." I smile at the thought of Aiden corralling a horde of teenage girls on the Metro from one place to another. "I love a girl who dreams big. Who does she look like?"

"If you're going off physical features, she could be my twin."

"You're proud of her."

"Unbelievably so," Aiden says. "She makes me want to be a better person. What about you? Any kids? Married?"

"No. Neither. I was married, once upon a time. I'm single, too."

"I think you're copying me. Doctor. Divorced. Single."

"Are you also not looking for a relationship? Because I've shunned dating for the foreseeable future."

"I'm not looking for a relationship either. You know how our profession is. Long hours, emotionally draining, and physically demanding. It doesn't award me—us—a lot of time to date."

I hum and decide to walk on a tightrope, a daredevil act with no safety net below. "Interesting. Two single people who don't want a relationship. A world of possibilities."

Oh, god.

I don't know what I'm saying or *why* I'm saying it, but I want to. A pressure in my chest swells at the idea of more time with Aiden, whatever that time might be.

Aiden's eyes darken, kerosene and flames emerging from behind the hazel. "My daughter told me I'm required to grab a coffee with the woman from the photo shoot after we finish. Is that something you'd be interested in, Maggie?"

My name has never sounded so sinister, so wicked, so right before. Is coffee a metaphor for something else? Some term I'm unfamiliar with because the only thing that's gotten me off lately is a rechargeable toy and my own two fingers? I swallow, not caring *what* it might be defined as, just that I want it.

"Coffee sounds great," I say. I can hardly recognize my voice. It's deep, full of need and desire and *no, I shouldn't*.

But, *fuck*, I really want to.

Aiden steps toward me and grins, another smile lobbed my way. I'm collecting them like little treasures and seashells found on a beach. His fingers reach out and tuck a rogue piece of hair behind my ear. His touch caresses down my cheek and he leans in, close to my ear, and whispers, "I was hoping you'd say that. I think we'll be great friends."

Breathing is impossible. A feat I'm unable to accomplish, too busy memorizing the wrinkles around his eyes. The shape of his lips, the drag of his hand down the curve of my face, the warmth of his body so near mine. I hear the sigh he emits, content and pleased, a ghost of a kiss against my skin.

"Mags, Aiden, we're all set up. Ready to start?" Jeremiah's voice is shrapnel cutting through the moment, slicing it in two.

"Yeah," I answer. "Be right there."

Distracting, distracting, distracting.

Aiden rests his palm on my lower back as we walk to the group. It's a solid weight, an anchor to keep me stable on shaky legs. We step around ring lights and backdrops, taking our time. His touch is unwavering, just *there*, a constant support.

He offers his hand to help lower me to the ground and waits until I'm fully seated to join me on the blanket. "I don't think I'm going to be able to get up," he says gruffly as he folds his legs. He winces and twists his back, the muscles under his sweater stretching. "There better be some damn good snacks in there."

I open the wicker basket and inspect the contents. "Sorry, no pickles. Just crackers and cheese."

"Unbelievable. Next time I do a fake picnic in an industrial building, I'm demanding some pickles. No one will ever want to work with me."

We distribute the food and make small talk, sharing our favorite ice cream flavors—mint chocolate chip for me, plain chocolate for him. How we feel about cold weather—Aiden is more of a summer guy. A discussion about movies arises; *Sweet Home Alabama* is, ironically, his favorite, and *Titanic* is mine. We have a ten-minute conversation dissecting the physics behind Rose not pulling Jack on the door.

The faces on set become blurred, movement shifting from in front of us to behind, adjusting lights and camera angles as they go. In between bites, a makeup artist bursts into our bubble, touching up a spot on my cheek with a fresh coat of blush. I know people are there, I'm aware of their presence, but in the moment, it's just me and Aiden, the rest of the world dissolving away.

He listens intently to my words, eyes never straying from my face. When a drop of strawberry jam lands on his finger, he licks it off. His tongue glides up the digit while never breaking my gaze, and I almost let out a strangled moan.

What else could he do with that tongue?

What else could he do to *me* with that tongue?

Turn me into a withering, spineless mess, probably. I'd be grateful, the sensible part of my brain giving way to lust and attraction, a convoluted flurry of satisfaction.

"Open up," Aiden says. His command is low and silky, exquisite velvet wrapped around my waist. My mouth parts, and he sets a cracker topped with cheese on my tongue. In a moment of bold spontaneity, of a woman in charge, I lick the pad of his thumb. He lets out a soft groan. "Dammit, Maggie," he mumbles. "You're driving me insane."

"A bad insane?" I ask. His eyes follow the bob of my throat as I swallow, and his jaw flexes with restraint. He looks like a man in pain, forced to control himself instead of doing what he really wants to do.

"Are you kidding me? A *good* insane. I feel like I'm losing my mind around you." His hand drops to my knee, palm splayed out over my jeans. His pointer and middle finger hook under my thigh, and he pulls me toward him. "Is this okay?"

No, I want to shout. *It's not nearly enough.*

"It's perfect," I say instead, content to soak up the remaining hours I get with Aiden Wood.

ELEVEN
AIDEN

JESUS CHRIST.

I really am losing my mind.

The feel of Maggie under my palm is intoxicating. It's like knocking back too many shots at the bar and trying to stand. Everything is a little hazy, a little wobbly, a little uneven. The world tilts, turning on its axis, and I tilt with it.

Her lip is caught in her teeth, eyes dancing with wonder. Her pulse drums under my thumb, and my grip tightens. I hear her breathing become shallower, a sure sign of attraction and arousal.

And, *fuck*, I'm turned on just touching her over her clothes. We're going to have a serious problem when we transition to the more intimate shots, because I'm not going to be able to hide how much I like her staring at me. I'm already hard, my dick stiffening in my briefs and making my jeans tight and uncomfortable. If she keeps looking at me with her mouth parted and her pupils blown wide, like she needs *me* to survive and is seconds away from launching herself into my arms, I'm a fucking goner.

"The chemistry between you two is sizzling." Jeremiah is

practically squealing. He bounces on his feet as he draws toward us, snapping an up-close shot.

"He has to be talking about you," I say to Maggie out of the corner of my mouth.

"You don't think you're sizzling?" Her head tips to the side. She's cute when she's inquisitive; her nose scrunches and her lips wiggle from side to side, contemplating.

"Nah. I'm a realist, not self-deprecating. Put the two of us side-by-side, and it's obvious you're the one carrying our good looks."

Maggie's laugh tumbles out of her like spilled wine. It's popped champagne at New Year's Eve with gold confetti around us, sticking to our sweat-covered skin. It's iridescent and all consuming, a sound I want—I *need*—to bottle up and replay on my worst days.

"I think we might be having our first fight as friends," she says.

"The first of many, I hope."

"Yeah." A nod and a smile, sure and certain, answer me. "I hope so, too. For what it's worth, Aiden, I think you're attractive."

"It's worth a lot. And I hope you know how beautiful you are." She blushes and dips her chin, hiding her eyes. *Well, that timidness won't do.* "Hey, Maggie. Look at me." Slowly, she complies. I bite the inside of my cheek to keep from slamming her lips onto mine, a reward for how well she listens. "You really are a stunning woman."

"Thank you," she whispers. "I'm not used to compliments, so it's a little foreign to hear so many in a row."

I frown. "I'm sorry. You deserve to hear them. And not just as a one-off, either. Frequently and often." I squeeze her thigh and let my hand move an inch up her leg. "You're definitely the hottest woman I've done a photo shoot with."

Maggie pushes my shoulder gently, palm lingering on my

arm. "What a terrible argument. I'm the only one you've done a photo shoot with."

"You haven't seen my *GQ* spread? The one where I wear my dinosaur tie the kids love? You're missing out."

"I know you're lying, but I'm picturing you with a dinosaur tie. It's really freaking cute."

"That part is true. I have a whole collection. It's a hit on the floor. Gotta find the good in every day, you know? Especially for those who have a hard time finding it for themselves. Sometimes it means wearing a silly tie with T-Rexes in top hats."

"You're a good man, Aiden Wood." Her hand moves to a box of candy hearts. She opens the package, extracting a few of the sugar pieces and reading the message. "This one says hottie. I haven't called anyone that since Y2K, but it's fitting. Your turn. Open up, Doc."

Fuck me.

New kink unlocked.

It takes effort to not let out the guttural moan taking up residence in my chest. No one's ever mentioned my profession during an intimate moment before. I never thought I'd be interested in hearing it, but now that I have? I might be obsessed.

"With pleasure," I murmur.

Two can play this game. Maggie rocked my world when she licked my thumb. It's time for some retribution.

She brings the snack to my mouth. I take the offering, my teeth grazing her finger and biting into the flesh. It's not hard enough to draw blood, but hard enough for her to know she has my attention. She's *had* my attention since I walked through the door and saw her for the first time.

Maggie hisses, the melody music to my ears. "Aiden." It's a whimper, like what I'm doing isn't enough.

"Tell me to stop." I take her hand and kiss her wrist, traces of sugar staining her skin. I kiss the underside of her arm, the spot just below her elbow. She's warm and smooth under my lips, the smell of oranges even more potent. "Tell me to stop, and I will."

"What if I don't want you to stop?" Her palm cups my cheek, pressing against my beard. "What if I asked you to keep going?"

"Then I would."

It's an easy answer. I don't know what, exactly, we're talking about, but it's all the same. Whatever she asks, I'll give her. If she wants my hand between her legs, I'll do it. She wants to sit on my face? Check. Does she want me to track down a cake for her? Consider it done.

She hums and her eyes sweep over my face. They travel from my eyebrows down to my nose, landing on my lips.

Ask me, I think.

Ask me to kiss you.

Maggie leans forward, and I go to meet her halfway.

Okay, *fuck*, we're doing this. With jam on my hand and a wicker basket poking my leg—not to mention tons of people watching us—I'm going to kiss this woman. Her hand falls from my cheek to my hip, settling there. I'm about to say something, about to whisper her name, when I hear a click and freeze.

"Okay." Jeremiah pulls out the Polaroid picture from his camera. Figures come into focus, developing from a dark square to one full of life and color. "How are you two feeling?"

I glance at Maggie and nod, letting her go first.

"Honestly? I'm kind of surprised how easy this is," she answers.

"Agreed," I chime in. I run my hand over my jaw and my eyes stay connected with hers. "It's fun when you have a good part-ner. I'm still not quite sure what to do with my hands, but I don't think I've made a total fool of myself."

"See for yourself," Jeremiah says. He hands the small photo to me. Maggie leans in, crowding my space, and I scoot closer to her.

"Maggie Houston." I whistle. "You're hot as hell."

"Hush." She touches my chest, fingers pressing into my skin. "You don't look like a fool at all." Her voice drops, speaking only to me. "You're hot as hell too, Doc."

Before I can come up with a quick-witted comment, Jeremiah is taking the photo back, tucking it into his pocket. "These scenes have gone very well. We have two options going forward. We can either call it a day, stop here, and head home. Or, we transition to the sexier part of the shoot. Clothes off, underwear on. We'll move to the bed. This might seem intimate, so I understand there could be hesitation at doing something that feels invasive and personal. It's not going to be my call. It's up to you."

I look at Maggie again. Our eyes meet and lock on each other. The idea of seeing her, *feeling her*, without clothes nearly sends me into a tailspin. I could run my hand up her leg. Revel in her breath on my bare skin. Everyone will see the fucking boner I'm rocking, but it would be worth it, to spend more time with her.

I lift my eyebrow, telling her I'm not going to be the one to make the decision.

She is.

TWELVE

MAGGIE

AIDEN and I rise to our feet. His mouth stays closed, deferring the decision to me. He might not speak, but his eyes reveal everything. I know what his answer would be. It's written out with his lapse in attention as his gaze falls to my hips. The flex of his fingers, like they want to grab my belt loops and tug me toward him. His hand adjusting the front of his jeans—*holy shit, he's hard*—and the curve of his lips into a pleased smile.

My head bobs up and down in slow motion, an eager confirmation of *yes, of course we can ditch our clothes*. It's an emphatic answer, and I hope my neck isn't jerking too violently as I think about how much of Aiden I'll get to see. Nerves are replaced with the overwhelming, debilitating notion that this... this jumping from an airplane without a parachute, free-falling from a cliff into ocean water, soaring over the craters of Earth on a glider sensation, feels *right*.

Excitement ripples through me. Color rises on my cheeks, not from embarrassment, but from sureness. From selfishness, finally doing something for myself.

I'm going to get to touch Aiden, and he's going to touch me, too. He'll probably be methodical and take his time, torturing me and shredding my self-control to pieces. I'm invigorated, spilled oil waiting to go up in flames, and Aiden is the one holding the match. I'm ready to welcome the heat.

"Hey," Aiden says. His voice is soft, and he's turned his back on the rest of the crew, shielding me from their eyes. It's just us, a private conversation. I'm protected and safe. His hand taps my elbow, fingers resting on the crook of my arm. "Are you sure? We can tap out."

"Do *you* want to tap out?" I ask.

Something dark flashes across Aiden's face. "I definitely do not want to tap out, Maggie, but I want to make sure you're okay with this."

We're delaying the inevitable. Either we touch each other here, in front of the cameras, or we touch each other when we walk outside. It's going to happen, an undeniable chemistry growing and building to a symphonic crescendo. I can feel it. He can feel it. Everyone watching us can feel it. It's been too long, and I know with absolute certainty it's Aiden Wood I want. I want him to run his hands up my stomach. I want his fingers to tug on my hair. I want him to make me feel like I'm the only one in the world, if only for a little while.

"I'm positive." My hand rests on his chest. Under my palm, I can feel his heart racing, the beat faster than a metronome. "I want this," I say with finality.

He cups my cheek, exercising care and consideration in the tilting of my chin, the thumb running down my jaw. "I want this, too." His protective timbre shifts to husky seduction. "Want me to go first? There's nothing good hiding under here, anyway."

I laugh, a tiny exhale of air. "Be my guest."

Aiden takes a step back, and my hand falls waywardly to my side as I force my gaze away. He pulls the sweater over his head. I hear the cable-knit land on the floor with a soft *plop*. "You can, uh, watch. We're going to be on a mattress together in a few minutes, so you might as well."

I let myself look. I drift from his face to his neck and chest. The skin previously covered by clothing is pale; a lighter complexion than the bottom half of his arms that see more sunlight. Freckles dot his shoulders and his chest, giving way to a trail of hair covering his stomach. He's made of soft skin, lines not hard and defined but smoother around the edges. I notice a lack of abdominal muscles, a little bit of weight around his middle where a cut V on other men would reside. It's less toned and more... *human*. When my attention catches on the scar extending from his hip bone to halfway up his torso, Aiden taps it with his fingers.

"Appendix removal when I was seven. Surgery went wrong, and I ended up with a nasty infection. It's one reason I wanted to go into the medical field," he explains. "In hopes that no one else would have a reminder of a poorly done job."

"Isn't it funny how such an infinitesimal moment can change the trajectory of your life?"

"Yeah." Aiden's eyes flick to mine. "Remarkable, really."

"Any tattoos?" I ask, further investigating his body.

"One. You can't see it unless I'm..." He trails off, leaving the sentence unfinished.

Naked.

The disyllabic word taunts me, a mocking of how it knows, but I don't. My hands want to grab the rest of his clothes and yank them off so I can find out. A hunt I'm ready to embark on, a treasure chest waiting for me at the end.

"Cool," I say, voice coiled tight.

Aiden kicks off his boots and pulls down his black socks. His fingers fumble with the button of his jeans. "Might as well keep going."

All I can offer is a pathetic nod. He unfastens the silver clasp, bringing the denim over his thighs and down his calves. The pants pool at his feet and he steps out, nudging them to the side. He's left in gray briefs that cling to his quads. There's definition to his legs, meticulously carved out from hours of standing on his feet. From climbing stairs at the hospital, I imagine, and kneeling to speak to young patients, dropping to their level so as not to appear intimidating.

The pretenses of privacy have vanished as I unabashedly stare and soak in the sight of him. They leave little to the imagination, clinging to his body like a second skin. His full length is outlined through the cotton and spandex materials, every vein and ridge of his shaft on display.

"Right." Heat pools in my stomach. "For what it's worth, you're wrong."

"Wrong about what, exactly?"

"There's plenty of good under there. Great, I'd even say."

His focus drops to the space between my jeans and my top where a tiny tease of skin shows. The heated gaze is an invitation to join him. I take off my shoes first. My hand shakes as I duel with the buttons on my shirt. It's impossible to separate the plastic from the satin.

"Do you need some help?" Aiden's voice is rough, a coarse piece of wood yet to be sanded. I nod and he steps nearer. The tips of his toes nudge against mine, announcing his arrival. His scent engulfs me, and I cocoon myself in the smell of cedar and pine. "Going to touch you now."

I nod again, words escaping me. I'm powerless as I note the pause of his touch as he patiently awaits my approval. When I grant it—*Aiden is going to touch me*—he smiles.

His deft fingers make quick work of the task. A button snags on a loose thread, and he brushes against the skin hidden beneath my clothes. I inhale sharply, the heat of his body mingling with mine, skin on skin contact. My top opens, baring my upper half to him. His large palms push the shirt down my shoulders until it falls, hitting the floor. I use his arm for balance as I step out of my jeans, shucking them out of sight.

The air is cooler without a layer of clothing to protect me from the draft in the room. I shiver, left standing in a tasteful forest green lingerie set. I'm covered, but the illusion is there. My breasts almost spill out. My nipples are barely concealed. If I stretched my arms behind me, the material would slip, revealing all of myself to him.

"Tada."

Aiden's eyes sweep across my face. A devastating wildfire blazes behind the hazel, and he hums his approval. The noise reverberates across my chest and settles between my legs.

"Maggie," he says. The tone is reserved for repenting sinners, making a deal with a deity for eternal salvation. And he's using it on *me*. "You are so beautiful."

THIRTEEN
AIDEN

"CAN I—" I start.

"Please," she says.

I look at her and soak her in, taking my time to rake over the luxurious lace decorating her body. It's green, a deep hue that brings out the brightness in her eyes. Her skin is tan, like she's spent hours on a beach or sailing the Mediterranean on a catamaran, letting the sun kiss her body and making it glow.

The triangle top cuts across her chest with exact precision. The fabric is thicker over her nipples so they aren't visible, but you can see the outline. The hint of rosy pink. The tease of pebbled peaks. My imagination runs wild, dreaming about how they would taste under my tongue or feel pinched between my fingers.

The top portion stretches halfway down her stomach, stopping well above her belly button. There I find the first spot of bare skin, unhidden by the scraps of material I want to rip off. Her stomach is slightly softer, morphing to a cinched waist and voluptuous hips. Sinister, wretched, *fuckable* things.

I wonder how they'd feel to hold. How they would look decorated with my fingerprints as she sinks onto me and controls the pace. Languid, intentional, slow to savor the moment.

Fucking wonderful, if I had to guess.

A pair of underwear covers her bottom half. It shows off some of her ass, classy, yet taunting. Breathing, I discover, is difficult. Erratic at best, and coming in through quick gulps.

Maggie seems to interpret my silence as disgust or disappointment. She shifts on her feet and folds her arms across her chest, a one-person hug to keep herself hidden.

"I'm, uh, I know I'm not—" She stops abruptly. My attention moves away from the dip of her thighs to her face. There's raw vulnerability in her eyes, a frown on her lips. "I haven't been to the gym in a while. I know I have love handles and some cellulite. My thighs touch, too."

It dawns on me, then. At some point in her life, Maggie has had to make herself appear smaller, less wonderful, to make others happy. And that makes my blood boil.

I blow out a breath and step closer. I place my hands on her shoulders, running my palms up and down her arms, erasing the goosebumps sprouting on her skin. "I'm going to tell you something embarrassing. It's vulgar, and you're going to have to forgive me, but you need to hear it."

Maggie nods and her lip quirks, the frown evaporating. "What is it?"

"I'm hard as hell, Maggie. Because of you. I'm dying a slow death being this close to you and not being able to do anything about it." She doesn't try to hide the glance down at my briefs. The obvious strain, the tightness I so badly want to relieve. All because of her. "Don't think for a second your body is anything less than goddamn perfect, because it is."

Before I can blink, her lips are pressing on my cheek, a kiss to my beard. "Thank you, Aiden."

I pat her shoulder. It's the least sexy move I've ever done in my entire life, but if I grip her hips like I want, if I touch her back and cup her ass like I want, I'm going to throw her on the bed, unable to control myself. Shoulders are safe, a neutral territory that won't get me in trouble and lead me to burying my face in her legs, burning the inside of her thigh with my stubble.

"Whenever you two are ready, we'll start." Jeremiah is kind this time, not rushing us along. "I'm only having three assistants help with these shots. I didn't want you two to feel overwhelmed."

I drop my forehead to hers. "Ready?"

"Yeah." She nods and finds my hand. "Ready."

Giving her palm a squeeze, we walk to the bed. Rose petals litter the sheets, and full-stemmed flowers are scattered across the pillows. I let her climb on first and keep my eyes on the floor instead of the swell of her ass as she bends over in front of me. She gets comfortable on the mattress, using her elbow to prop herself up. I sit on the edge and swing my legs over, lying parallel to her. Jeremiah moves to the foot of the bed, with one of his assistants remaining on the side. Another woman leans over and arranges Maggie's hair out of her face before stepping back and disappearing.

"Hey," I say. There's a rose with a stem full of thorns close to her arm. I brush it away so she doesn't get hurt.

"Hi." Maggie smiles.

"Want to hear something pathetic?"

"Always."

"I haven't been in bed with a woman in almost five years," I admit.

"Really? I'm surprised. I thought maybe you'd... I don't know, be some womanizer. The hit of the school pickup line."

"This really appeals to the ladies." I pat my stomach. "Who needs Joe from the gym when you could have this?"

Maggie knocks my hand out of the way. Her palm rests flush

across my skin. "It appeals to me," she says earnestly. The compliment feels like I just won a fight, a knockout round that wasn't even close and I'm the champion of the ring. "I'm waiting for the joke, though. You haven't been with a woman in bed, but you have in your car."

"Car? Who the hell owns a car in D.C.?"

"You know what I mean."

"Nope. Nada. Zero. I told you, I'm not looking for a relationship."

"Sex doesn't have to include a relationship."

"Maggie Houston, are you propositioning me?" I tut and shake my head. "I'm appalled."

"You are such a—hey!" She squeals as I lift her, picking her up and plopping her down on my thighs.

Whatever sarcastic comment she's going to hurl my way dies in her throat. She looks down at me, and there's passion there. In her eyes, on her lips. The slight rock of her hips and how hard I have to bite my tongue to keep from letting out a strangled sound.

Five years. Five long, lonely years. I'm not going to fuck Maggie here so everyone can watch. I'm selfish; if that's a possibility, I want to be the only one to experience the sounds she makes and the way she looks naked under the light of the moon. But simply having a woman look at me like she wants me, *touching* me, is soul awakening.

I've kind of been faking my confidence up to this point through jokes and banter, hoping she doesn't see through the facade of nerves and how worried I was about fucking something up for her friend. After hearing how important Jeremiah is to Maggie, it made me want to go all in, to fully commit to doing things right. But now? Now, I'm not pretending. She's still looking at me, I'm still looking at her, and I wish we were anywhere else because I'm desperate, going fucking *mental* at knowing she's so close and not being able to do anything about it.

"What are you thinking?" she asks. I can't hear any clicks of the cameras, and I think Jeremiah is exerting serious patience, letting us ease into these new roles before starting his snapshots.

"I'm thinking about how much I want to do to you—with you—but I can't."

"What if you could do something about it?" Maggie leans forward, her hands landing on either side of my shoulders. Her hair covers her face, a curtain shielding her eyes, and I tuck a strand behind her ear. "Tell me what it would be."

"I'd bring you closer. I'd touch your thighs. Your neck. Your ass. I'd see how well your breast fit in my hand."

The words spill out, my tongue loose, my inhibitions lowered. I expect her to pull away, to shut this down and end everything right here, right now.

But she doesn't. She bends to my ear and whispers, "Then do it."

FOURTEEN
MAGGIE

AIDEN MOVES AS FAST as a viper going for a kill.

He shifts our position. He drags me up his lap and my legs wrap around his waist. His hands rest on my back, between the valley of my shoulder blades, running his palm up and down my spine.

"Good?" Aiden asks. The lines between acting and reality are becoming blurred, a hazy outline I no longer care to decipher, because this right here? This is as real as the sun rising and the sky being blue.

I'm distracted as his hand moves to my arm, trailing over my elbow and across the top of my chest. He's painting me like an artist would. I'm his canvas, his muse, the object of his blistering affection. My exhale is shaky, barely controlled. His touch metabolizes me to a bundle of nerves. A puddle of want.

"Yes," I whisper back. My eyes close and I give into the sensation. I give in to *him*. The scent of his cologne. The press of his hard length against the inside of my thigh. The scratch of his beard, rough against my neck. An unfortified realization of how *wonderful* all of this is.

He initiated the contact, but I want to make him feel good,

too. I drag myself forward half an inch, our hips almost fusing together, and a low hiss escapes his mouth.

"*Fuck*, Maggie."

It's not an admonishment, but a drawn-out exclamation of pleasure. He's seconds away from begging me to do it again. We're two magnets joining, an unavoidable bond. The chemistry, the heat from late morning and early afternoon reaching an apex of pent-up passion expanding in the two inches of free space between us.

It's not enough. I fuse our bodies together in earnest now, two becoming one. My nipples graze his chest. His hand slots into mine, intertwining our fingers. Our hips align, only scraps of clothing separating us from fully uniting. It's a puzzle piece fitting perfectly in place.

"You feel so good, sweetheart."

I latch onto the praise, the endearment awakening a secret part within me. I'm wet, so fucking wet for this kind, sweet, devilish man. My fingers sift through his hair, tugging on his scalp, and Aiden lets out a growl.

"If there weren't any cameras here," he continues, lips blazing a tantalizing path down the column of my throat, "if there wasn't an audience watching us..."

"What would you do?" I ask. It's a prod and a push, a nudge to get him to be specific in his verbal pursuit. It's how we got here in the first place, a move I do not regret.

"I'd take your bra off. I'd slide your underwear down next, taking my time until you were naked and at my mercy. Then, I'd worship your body. I'd wrap your legs around my neck and bury my face between your thighs." His thumb catches on my bottom lip, pulling it down. "I'm starving, and I want to feast on you."

I'm going to detonate. I'm alight with nerves, seconds away from combusting as lust and desire rattle my brain.

"You like my body?"

I need to hear it again, to know that the first time wasn't a fluke, designed so we'd end up here.

Aiden pulls back to look at me, eyes hooded. "No. I fucking love your body. It deserves to be worshiped and adored. These hips." He runs his hands up my thighs, snapping the waistband of my underwear against my skin. "Your chest." His eyes dip to the straps of my top. The right side has slid down, hooking near my elbow. "I want to lay you out and study you, Maggie, committing every line and dip and curve to memory so I can confirm my suspicions. Every inch of you is beautiful. And if you were mine, I'd remind you of that every second of every day. Through my words. With my hands. With my mouth. With my eyes. Repeatedly, until the message stuck."

"You're making me want to forget that we're never going to see each other again." I roll my hips and Aiden drops his forehead to my shoulder, groaning, a soft sound I scoop up. Somewhere, a camera clicks. Somewhere, a light moves, shifting from bright to dark, the ambiance changing. Somewhere, another brick falls, and another, and another, and another. Seven billion people in the world, and all I see is him.

"I think I'm seconds away from kissing you," he whispers into the shell of my ear.

"Do it," I answer.

"Are you sure?"

"Yes."

I've never been more sure of anything in my life. A single word, about to change everything. His mouth hovers above mine, waiting for me to pull back.

I don't.

I lean in further, a hair's breadth away from him. My lips part in invitation, and there's only milliseconds before he crashes into me, devouring me whole.

Aiden Wood kisses like a man possessed, someone living

their last day on Earth. The kiss isn't gentle. It's rough and wild, a tornado of limbs, the scrape of teeth, the swipe of tongues. My arms drape around his neck, tugging him closer. He huffs out a chuckle. His left hand cups my cheek and his right slides under my ass.

There's the temptation to ask him to keep going. To slip under the material and see how wet I am. To not stop, but take and take and *take*. His hand moves from my cheek to my rib, large palm splayed out over my stomach. An opportunity is being presented to me, and I jump on it.

"I haven't been keeping track of your game."

"No?" Aiden asks. "Something distracting you?"

"You could say that. If I had to guess, though, you have one question left." I pull away so I can look him in the eyes. "What's it going to be?"

There's no hesitation, no pause to consider what he might want to ask. It's quick, the idea already in his head.

"Would you like to come to my house after this? I can't lie and say that I haven't felt something between us, because I have. And I don't want it to end soon."

There it is.

And, as quick as he asks, I answer.

"Yes. I need you, Aiden. Badly."

His mouth moves to my neck and bare shoulder. "You should know what you're getting into if you come back to my place. I'm going to want more. Everything. All of it, Maggie. All of you. Do you still want to say yes?"

I nod my head so fast, my neck cramps up. "Yes. A thousand times yes."

"Thank god. I need to get you out of these clothes immediately."

"But we're in agreement about no relationships, right?"

"Right." Some of his bravado momentarily slips before he smiles again. "It's a one-night thing. That's it."

'Twenty-four hours," I propose.

"Even better. I'll cook you dinner. Then I'll eat you out on my counter."

My face flames. It takes effort to not slip my hand down my underwear. To relieve some of the ache building there. "I don't need dinner," I manage to get out.

"Yes," Aiden says firmly. "You do."

"Can I run home and grab some things? And I need to send your address to Lacey so she has my location. You know, because of the whole hooking up with a stranger thing."

"Of course. Safety first. I'll give you the door code, too, so she has it. Any food allergies?"

"Nope."

Aiden grins and leans forward, a soft kiss pressed to my lips. This one is reverent, sweet. "Get ready for the best twenty-four hours of your life, Maggie."

FIFTEEN
AIDEN

THE SHOOT WRAPS up forty-five minutes later. Maggie and I don't kiss again, but we're not cold to each other. There's a mutual understanding in place; everything can wait until we get back to my apartment. We exchange phone numbers, and I give her my address as we pull our clothes back on. I tell her to call if she gets lost.

I stop by the market on my way home and pick up some things for dinner. On an impulse, I grab a bouquet of poppies, too, not overthinking why I feel inclined to buy her pretty flowers when I'm going to have her bent over a chair later tonight.

Now that I'm walking through my apartment, yanking off my coat and putting a fresh set of sheets on the bed, I don't expect her to show up. In the time we've been apart, she's probably come to her senses. Her friend probably told her it was a bad idea. It's not entirely wrong; a night with someone you don't know? It could be disastrous.

Maybe she only agreed because she was trying to be nice, to find an out from the conversation, not because she *wanted* to.

Caught up in the moment of temporary lust, all rationality swept away.

Sure, her hands were tugging my hair and her breath was coming out in short pants. Yeah, her eyes fluttered closed and her thighs locked around my middle with a surprising amount of force. But, ending up outside my door in twenty minutes seems implausible. A fever dream, one I'll believe when I see.

I dump a box of pasta into the boiling water on the stove and check the oven for the meatballs I bought because I remembered they are her favorite food. I'm not delusional; I'm well aware this isn't a date. It's two adults having a night together where we both get off and never see each other again. I still want her to be comfortable, though. Fed and warm. Relaxed. I want to peel off the lingerie she was wearing earlier with my teeth, but I also don't want her to pass out from hunger. A couple of crackers at the shoot isn't enough to last the whole night, and if she's coming to my house, I'm going to take care of her.

I turn the burner down to let the sauce simmer. Checking the time, I swap the meatballs in the oven for a loaf of garlic bread. There's only five minutes until she'll be here—allegedly—and all of this will be real. Really *fucking* real.

My phone rings on the counter, and I snatch it up. Disappointment blazes through me when I see Shawn's face on the screen.

"What?" I answer with unintended hostility. I prop the device in the crook of my neck and grab a spoon to stir the pasta.

"Hello to you, too. What's got you all pissy?"

"Nothing."

"Do you want to meet for drinks? Or hang at your place? Maven's at Katie's, right? I want to hear how today went."

"I'm kind of busy."

There's a long stretch of silence before Shawn speaks again. I know I've shocked him by having plans. "With what?"

"I'm having a woman over, okay? And I don't want you to say shit, because you're going to make this a bigger deal than it is. We agreed to spend one night together. That's it. So save the hopeless romantic diatribe. It's sex. Nothing more."

"*What?*" Shawn's exclamation is so loud, I have to pull the phone away from my ear.

"Don't," I warn him.

"I'm not allowed to celebrate my best friend getting laid for the first time in—hang on. Four years, eleven months and eight days?"

"You have a calendar that tracks when I last had sex? You fucking creep."

"Hard not to when you set the record for world's longest dry spell. Don't bullshit me, Aiden. I want details."

"It's Maggie."

"Maggie?" he repeats. "From the shoot?"

"Yeah. We hit it off. Things got heated. I asked if she wanted to spend the night, and she agreed. Now I'm making her dinner, freaking the fuck out, and wondering if eight condoms is enough, because I'm going to look like a fucking loser who only lasts six seconds because I haven't had a woman on top of me in half a decade. Jesus, this was a stupid idea."

"Aiden. You know you're not a loser, right? I'm just giving you shit about the whole dry spell thing."

"I know. I'm just... She's special, Shawn. Wicked smart. Funny. Sexy as hell. I know it's only one night, but I don't want to mess anything up. I want things to be good for her."

"Best advice? Take everything in stride. Who cares if you have sex on the couch or in your room? You're spending time with a woman you think is amazing. That's awesome, man."

"In stride. Okay. I can do that."

"Why only one night?"

"We both not looking for a relationship. This is what she

wants, and it's what I want, too. It's easier. No logistical night-mares, but we still get to fool around."

"Okay. As long as you two are on the same page."

"Yeah. We are."

"Good. Okay. I'll let you go. Man. I can't believe you're getting laid tonight and I'm going to sit at home by myself. What the hell do I do?"

"Wow. One night without sex. How will you survive?" A knock on the door startles me. "Shit. I have to go."

"Have fun, man! Call me tomorrow."

I hang up and put my phone in my pocket, walking across the living room and pausing at the door. Two quick breaths, and I turn the knob.

There's Maggie. Her cheeks are flushed from the cold, and she's wearing a dress that hits above her knees. Boots are on her feet, and a jacket covers her arms. Her hair is thrown up in a messy bun, and tendrils of honey-colored strands frame her face.

It feels like the wind gets knocked out of me. She's so beau-tiful. Even with a fresh face—the makeup from earlier wiped away and a tired haze flickering in her eyes—she's breathtaking.

"Hey," I say, offering her a smile. I'm the first to speak, a task I think is needed to show I want her here.

"Hi," she answers, returning my smile.

"Want to come inside?"

"Yeah. I do."

I step back and let her pass by. "I can take your coat and bag."

She shimmies out of the black wool, and I hang it on the rack adjacent to the door with her overnight tote. She's left in a short-sleeved navy blue dress. The material hugs her chest and waist, fanning out over her legs. I feel like an asshole for dressing so casual, choosing a pair of gray joggers and a black shirt instead of jeans.

"You look great, Maggie."

"Thanks." She tucks a piece of rogue hair behind her ear. "It seemed a little counterproductive to put on more clothes after having so little on earlier, but I'm not sure the people on the Metro wanted to see me in my underwear."

Her eyes sweep over the foyer and the rest of the space. I wonder how my apartment looks through her eyes. I didn't have enough time to clean up before she got here, and the place is a little chaotic. The blankets on the couch aren't folded. Maven's backpack is unzipped, a planner and folder spilling onto the floor. A stack of unopened mail is about to fall off the kitchen island.

"Wow, Aiden. This is really nice," she says. "I like that it looks like a home. It's spacious and way bigger than my place. And look at those windows. Floor-to-ceiling. I'm impressed."

"The higher rent is worth the splurge to not stumble over Maven in the morning. She can be a terror before six a.m. Sorry about the mess. I don't, uh, typically do this sort of thing."

"You don't invite random women back to your house for what you think will be mind-blowing sex?"

I laugh and shake my head. "No. You'll have to forgive me for not having things organized. Ignore the dishes in the sink and the swimsuit hanging from the door handle down the hall."

"I didn't come over to count how many categories of towels you have in your linen closet."

"You didn't? Why did you come over, Maggie?"

The moment shifts. The brief stint of awkward conversation wanes. There's a spark in the air now. Before I can blink, before I can take a breath, before I can ask another question, Maggie launches herself at me. I'm ready and anticipate her attack with open arms. I catch her, and her legs wrap around my waist. It's soul-crushing, nearly suffocating, but who the fuck needs oxygen anyway when I can survive solely on the taste of her lips against mine?

I move us, blindly stumbling through the living room until her back collides with the window overlooking the city below.

"Is it crazy to say I missed you?" she whispers. Her head tilts, resting against the glass. I take advantage of the angle, my lips working away from her mouth down her throat. I find the patch of skin I got a sample of earlier and have been craving since she's been gone.

"No," I grind out. "I missed you, too." I bunch her dress at her waist. My grip changes, cupping her ass with both of my hands. Her cheeks are warm under my touch, incredibly smooth like the rest of her body. The swell of her backside fits perfectly in my palms, and a hint of lace teases my knuckles. I groan, nipping at her neck, below the shell of her ear. "I really fucking missed you."

She kisses me again, tongue dancing with mine. I palm her breast, massaging it with my hand. Maggie moans, her thighs squeezing tightly around me. Her fingers work under the waistband of my joggers, and I rock my hips forward, hoping she can feel how hard I already am for her.

"Aiden?" she whispers. "Is something burning?"

"Shoot." I pull us away from the wall and slide Maggie down my body. "Be right back."

I hustle to the kitchen, shove on some oven mitts, and pull out the garlic bread. A waft of smoke rushes my face, and I bat it away. Half of the loaf is burnt, but the other is salvageable.

"You made dinner." Maggie slides onto one of the barstools, watching me move around the kitchen.

"I'm trying to. Sorry about the smell." I open the window over the sink a quarter of an inch. "I was distracted."

"I'll take the blame. What are you making? Can I help with anything?"

"Spaghetti and meatballs. I hear it's a favorite."

"Aiden," she whispers. She jumps off the leather and walks to me, wrapping her arms around my shoulders. "You made that for me?"

I shrug and hold her waist, hoping I didn't overdo it. "Yeah. It's not a big deal. Full disclosure: The meatballs are frozen and the sauce is from a jar. Don't judge my cooking based on the limited time I had to get ready."

She laughs and kisses me softly. I run my hand up her back, between the her shoulder blades, ending at the nape of her neck. My fingers curl, giving her a gentle squeeze. "I'm sure it'll taste great."

"Do you want something to drink? Beer? Wine? Water? We never got to the beverage preferences in our game."

"Gin and tonic is my go-to, but water is perfect."

I release her, regrettably, and pour a glass from the fridge. "The pasta is finished. Give me two minutes, and we can eat."

"Take your time. Watching a man cook is sexy." Maggie's gaze catches on the vase full of red, pink, and yellow poppies. "Oh, those are beautiful."

"Those are for you."

"For me?" she squeaks.

"I picked them up on the way home. There's a guy down the road who sells them. They were too nice to pass up. Might as well lean into the whole Valentine's Day cliché."

Her eyes soften. "You're my favorite one-night stand ever, Aiden, and we haven't had sex yet. Thank you."

I reach over and give her hip a squeeze. I'm tempted to lift her dress and sink to my knees. I want to kiss the spot above the waistband of her underwear, then the inside of her thigh.

"You're very welcome. Hope I can keep the title the rest of the night. Ready to eat?"

"God, yeah. Those crackers today were hardly enough food. I'm famished."

"C'mon. Food. Dessert. Bedroom. In that order."

"I recall someone promising to eat me out on the counter. Does the offer still stand?" She gives me a wink. Her teeth sink into her bottom lip and her hips sway as she walks back to her chair.

I tilt my head toward the ceiling and close my eyes.

Fuck.

Eight condoms definitely won't be enough.

SIXTEEN

MAGGIE

"JARRED SAUCE OR NOT, this is delicious," I say. "You didn't mention you were a cook."

"I threw pasta in a pot of boiling water." Aiden laughs, wiping some marinara from the corner of his mouth. "I'm hardly a professional."

"Still. It's impressive."

"All this flattery is going to go to my head. It's easy to fall into the cycle of takeout after a long day at work, but cooking for a teenage athlete reminds me to avoid the burgers and fries and make a meal that's fairly healthy once in a while. All set with your plate?"

"Yeah. I can do the dishes."

"Absolutely not. I'm going to toss them in the sink with the rest of the pile and worry about them tomorrow. Give me a few minutes, and then I'm all yours. Feel free to take a look around while you wait."

I jump off the barstool. "Is this my chance to snoop? To see what's hiding in your sock drawer?"

"Now I wish I had something cool in there besides socks

with tacos and cats on them. Come back in here when you're done, then we'll eat some dessert."

"Do you mind if I take my shoes off?"

"This place is yours for the next twenty-four hours, Maggie. You can do whatever you want."

I grin and unzip my knee-high boots, leaning them against the counter next to a pair of shoes that must be Aiden's. "Whatever I want?"

His eyes blaze and he pulls me toward him, capturing my lips in a searing kiss. "Whatever you want."

He gives my ass a tap and I walk down the hallway to the left of the kitchen. Photos flank the walls and I stop to peer at them. There's Aiden, his arm around a guy with tattoos. That must be Shawn, the best friend. Next is a framed photograph of him with a young girl. She's on his shoulders and they're both laughing. It must be his daughter; she's nearly identical to him. There are a dozen more; Aiden graduating from med school. A family portrait. A trip to a ski resort.

I spy a door at the end of the hall, partially ajar. I push it open and smile. Aiden's bedroom. Complete with curtains, a head and footboard, and a king mattress. A shirt hangs from the edge of the laundry basket. A baseball hat is on the door handle to the bathroom. There are a couple big windows and a rug under the bed. It's clean and well-organized, the space of an adult man who has his life together.

He said I could look, so I boldly walk inside. It smells like him; woodsy, with a hint of spice. The walls are a faded white. There are more pictures in here. One on the bedside table next to a glass of water. The other on the large dresser by a half-burnt candle. Both are of him with his daughter, the biggest smile I've ever seen plastered on his face.

It's hard to ignore how much I'm enjoying spending time with Aiden. He's not the first guy to give me any attention; I've had patients' family members flirt with me while I try to give a diagnosis. A cute guy in the coffee shop striking up casual conversation. A man who lives in my building, offering me a smile in the elevator. Aiden is different, though. Knowing he's watching me, cooking for me, and buying me flowers is more... impactful.

Even with an end date carved in stone, he's respectful. He's not forcing me on my knees or yanking my dress off the second I walk through the door. It's methodical, a process to his plan. And, *god*, the kisses he's showered me with tonight are far better than anything at the photo shoot. They're hotter, a promise behind them. When he lifted me and carried me to the wall, I almost melted on the spot, a precursor to what else will be coming my way.

I notice a white coat hanging in his closet. I move toward it, curious to see if the hospital where he works is written on the polyester. It goes past our boundaries of *strangers*, but I can't help wondering. My fingers curl around the knob when I hear footsteps behind me.

I turn around to find Aiden leaning against the door frame to his room. He smiles and crosses his arms over his chest. I wonder if he knows he has a drop of marinara on his forehead.

"How's the snooping going?" he asks.

"I'm disappointed. I was expecting to find much juicier things."

"What can I say? I'm a boring, middle-aged man. I don't bring a whole lot to the table."

"Not true. You can cook boxed pasta. That's more than a lot of men can say."

"Fair." He reaches his hand out. I forget about the lab coat and make my way over to him. He pulls me into a hug and I sigh in his embrace, content. "Want some dessert? Sorry to be the voice of reason, but I thought we could eat some ice cream and talk about expectations for tonight. I'm all for spontaneity, but as someone who got a tattoo they regret to this day, I want to make sure we're on the same page."

"Am I finally going to get to see this famed tattoo?"

"Only if you remember that I was incredibly intoxicated when I asked for it and you don't hold it against me."

"I'll do my best to be a neutral party, but no promises."

We walk hand-in-hand down the hallway, pausing briefly so Aiden can show off the picture from Maven's state swim meet last year, where she won the one-hundred-meter freestyle. He's so animated when he talks about her, with twinkling eyes and a full heart. It's infectious, that love. It swallows you whole and reminds you of all the good left in the world. You don't hear many people talk so emphatically and passionately about someone they care for these days. But Aiden? He gushes over his child's achievements, so proud of everything she's accomplished. It makes him even more attractive.

I take a seat on the stool again, and he scoops us out some ice cream. Mint chocolate chip, I notice, and I bite back a grin when he hands over my glass bowl.

"We both agree this is just for tonight. When you leave tomorrow, we won't try to hunt the other down," he starts. He eats a spoonful and winces, clearly experiencing a mild bout of brain freeze.

"Anything that happens in here, we keep to ourselves. Within reason, of course. I don't know if your best friend is going to ask for details like mine, but no kink-shaming allowed after the fact. If we agree to something, we respect the privacy of the other when all is said and done."

"Brilliant. You know how long it's been for me since I've been with someone. If you feel comfortable—"

"Four years. No one since I've been divorced."

A solar flare of possessiveness kindles behind Aiden's eyes.

"Fuck, Maggie. It might make me an asshole for being glad you've gone unsatisfied for so long, but it's hot as fuck I'm going to be the first to touch you. Now—Expectations. Sex, obviously. I hate to make this sound so clerical when all I want to do is toss you on my bed, but I don't want to do anything that crosses a firm boundary you have."

I push my ice cream around with my spoon and hunch my shoulders. "I'm not sure I can tell you that."

He pauses and peers at me. "Okay," he says gently, waiting for more.

"It's because I don't know what firm boundaries I might have."

SEVENTEEN

AIDEN

SHIT.

Did I massively fuck up? Read into this way more than I should have? She was married, so I assumed she was experienced. Now I'm second-guessing everything.

And *Maggie*. Her confidence wavers and the calm, cool demeanor splinters, an emotion akin to shame taking over. The swagger she had when she leapt into my arms is gone. She curls in on herself, and this is the farthest away she's felt from me all day. I'm not sure what I'm supposed to say or do. Apologize? Wait? Be the first to speak?

Fuck it. I don't like seeing her like this. I'm going in.

"Hey." I keep my voice soft and reach across the island to find her hand. I lace her fingers through mine and give her palm a squeeze. "Are you okay?"

"Yes." It's curt, a sweeping dismissal. She's obviously *not* okay, but I'm not going to push it. Her chin dips and her eyes dart away, focusing on the crumbs left behind from the number we did on the garlic bread. "It's embarrassing to say."

"There's no judgment in this house. You're allowed to like whatever you want."

"It's not that." She scoots her chair closer to mine. I use my other hand to rub soothing circles on her knee, over the fabric of her dress. I hope it conveys some sort of assurance that she's safe here. "Promise to not make fun of me?"

"I promise, sweetheart."

"I was married for five years. Throughout my marriage, sex was only used to try and get pregnant. It was always planned, sticking to the same routine every time. He never made me come. He never went down on me. We never tried anything out of the box. There's so much I think I might like, but I'm not sure."

"He... he never made you come?" I ask through clenched teeth. "He just finished and that was that?"

Maggie nods. "Yeah. I'd suggest different positions I thought would be hot after reading them in my books, and he'd roll his eyes. He'd call them dirty or say he didn't understand the point. Sex is sex, no matter how it's done. Why bother being adventurous?"

My hand lifts, and I bring it to the curve of her cheek. It dances over to the plump lips covered in firehouse red, a darker, more sensual shade than this afternoon. "You bother being adventurous because what your woman wants, your woman gets. No questions asked. He never tasted you, Maggie? Never ate you out until you were begging to finish? Never wore your come on his mouth like a goddamn prize?"

Maggie's breathing shifts. Pink blossoms on her chest, and her eyes glaze over. "No."

"He never fucked you from behind and watched the way your perfect ass bounced as you sank onto his dick?"

"Never," she whispers. Her thighs open, and the pink from her cheeks moves down to her chest.

"And he never got to feel your pussy clench around his fingers? Never brought you to the edge again and again with his tongue, demanding one more out of you until you were so spent, your limbs were useless?"

Words fail her this time. A soft, long moan is my answer as she shakes her head.

I lean forward. "Good," I whisper in her ear. My lips graze her throat, down her neck. "That means I get to be your first in practically everything. A title I'm honored to have, and one I'll make very worth your while." Maggie's hand folds over mine, and she brings my palm on a slow path from her knee to her upper thigh. I know what she's trying to convey, and it kills me to say no. "In a minute, sweetheart. I promise I'll give you what you deserve. What you need. But first, you need to tell me everything you've ever wanted to try. Tell me what else he never did, because we're going to check them all off tonight."

"I can make a list." The pitch of her voice is five octaves higher than before. "I can write them down."

"Do you want a pen and paper? Or to use your phone?"

"Paper, please."

I drop a kiss on her forehead. "Coming right up." I stand and open the junk drawer, rummaging around for a pad of paper and a pencil. I sift through old batteries, a participation award from Maven's science fair three years ago, finally finding what I need. "Here you go."

"There are things I've read about but I'm not sure I'll actually like in real life. When I'm reading them on the pages, I get turned on. I touch myself." She picks up the pencil then sets it down. Her fingers drum on the lined notepad, nervous. "I also don't expect you to want to do all of them. Or any of them, for that matter."

"Trust me, Maggie. I'm going to want to do them."

"What do you like?"

"Right now, I like you. And all that comes with it. More specifically? I'm very open minded. The only things I say no to are blood play, scenarios that would involve physically hurting you, and animals. And, for tonight, sharing. It might take me some time for me to get back in the groove, and I can't promise I have the stamina I did ten years ago, but there's plenty of time. Besides, I don't need my cock inside you to make you come, angel. Write down everything you've ever thought about."

Maggie nods and spins on the stool, staring at the paper straight on. I can tell she's determined. Her jaw sets. Her nose scrunches. Her brows wrinkle and her lips bow into a frown. I want her to be honest and forthcoming with me, but I don't want this to feel like *work*.

I stand and move from my stool so I'm behind her. She starts to write, and I kiss the apple of her cheek. Remembering the way her face flushed at the shoot when I praised her, I can almost guarantee that's going to be included. "Good start," I say softly. I pull her hair free from her bun, and push the waves to the side. I kiss her neck, letting my mouth linger in each spot before finding a new inch to explore. Her hand falters on the paper before resuming her writing.

"You're distracting," she whispers as she marks down *spanking* and *being told what to do*.

Perfect timing.

"Open your legs." She inhales and adjusts her position on the leather. She leans back into me, back resting against my chest, and parts her thighs. "You listen so well, Maggie."

The hook of the g in *degradation* goes wonky. "This one I'm not sure about."

I push her dress up to her hips, the same skin I saw earlier today greeting me. I rest my hand on her inner thigh, near her pelvis, and draw a circle. "Care to elaborate?"

"I don't want you to call me a whore. But I... I want to do something embarrassing. Crawling, I think."

"Noted. You underlined exhibitionism twice."

"I did? Oh. Today when we were kissing in front of everyone, I imagined them watching us do more than kiss and I liked it."

"You thought about them watching as I took off your underwear and slid a finger inside you." I drag my hand further up her thigh, resting on the line of her underwear. "You wanted them to see you choke on my cock, didn't you, and see how deep you could get?"

"Yes."

It's so quiet, but so sincere. My dick hardens. So far, I'm game for everything she's listed, and I plan to deliver on all of them. Exhibitionism might be the hottest one. I adjust the bulge in the front of my joggers and Maggie's back arches as my length juts against her spine.

"Hard for you, Maggie." I kiss her neck and bring the strap of her dress down. A fire-engine red bra peeks out. "You're so fucking sexy."

"I-I think I'm finished."

Picking up the paper, I read the items she's written. Light bondage. Blindfold. Showering together. Spanking. Degradation. Blowjob. Praise. Exhibitionism. Her on top.

Easy. Done.

I spin her stool so she's facing me. I tilt her chin and kiss her lips. "You are so hot. Why don't you get on the counter, sweetheart?"

"The counter? Why?"

"You're tense and nervous. I'm going to take the edge off." It takes a moment, but Maggie seems to understand what I'm asking. She stands and jumps onto the marble, looking at me for her next set of directions. I tilt my head to the side. "Try again, Maggie."

"What?" She frowns. "What did I do wrong?"

"You want the world to see you, don't you? Face the windows

and spread your legs. I didn't get to finish my dessert, and now the whole city can watch while I do."

EIGHTEEN
MAGGIE

MY HEART RACES in my chest and my hands tremble in my lap. A bead of sweat slides down my spine, catching in the waistband of my underwear. Aiden left no mystery to his words, the intent clear and concise. Here, in front of the floor-to-ceiling windows that look out to the city, where anyone in neighboring buildings can see, he's going to go down on me.

I swallow my moan. This is exactly why I came over. This is what I want, what I've *craved*. I knew there wouldn't be anything sweet or quiet about being with Aiden. It's going to be loud, earth-shattering, and so vastly different from the prim and proper sex I've had in the past.

Until I got into reading, I didn't think men wanted to go down on their women. Parker never went down on me, not once. Even getting him to do anything with my breasts was like pulling teeth. A chore, one he was *forced* to do. And here's Aiden, asking me to lie down on his countertop like I'm a buffet he's going to devour.

I nod—I think? Maybe I don't. Maybe my body moves on its own volition. I pivot on the gray surface and scoot to the other side, the distance from him feeling like miles.

"Like this?" I'm staring out the glass. Across the street, on the other side of the block, I see a couple setting the table for dinner. In the unit below them, a dog is curled up in a bed. I catch sight of my reflection and see my chest heaving. I look wrecked, and we haven't started yet.

"Yeah," he answers. It's breathless, and he walks so he's positioned between my legs. His hands land on my knees, and he gently nudges my thighs apart. "Fuck, Maggie. You're so sexy."

"Should I—how do you want me?"

"Lie back and relax. Open your legs. Let me see that pretty pussy of yours."

I've entered a catatonic state. My soul leaves my body and I'm watching from above, turned on and nearly frantic. I wiggle my hips and lie back, my shoulder blades connecting with the surface beneath me.

His hand runs up my thigh, from my knee to my hip. He hikes my dress up so my bottom half is on display for Aiden—and the world—to see. I let out a breath. His fingers toy with the underwear I'm wearing, and he runs his palm over the lace, pressing his heel into my clit and rubbing once.

I moan. My back arches off the countertop and my legs fall apart, completely open, completely bared to him. The sound echoes through the quiet room, magnified.

"I like the red." Aiden presses a kiss to my knee and shoves my underwear to the side. I hear an inhale, then a barrage of expletives. His grip on my hip tightens, fingers pressing into my skin hard enough to leave a mark. I hope they do.

"Aiden," I whimper. My hand reaches for his arm, finding his shoulder. "Please."

"Please what?"

"Please touch me."

"You're going to have to be more specific than that. If you want something, Maggie, you can tell me."

"Please make me come. Finger me. I don't care, I just need you." I'm panting now, scarily close to begging.

"I like hearing you say my name. But I'd like it even more if you screamed it." His finger runs through my slit, enough to tease, enough to taunt, but not enough to satisfy. "Such a beautiful pussy. Look how wet you are. Your underwear is soaked."

"More. More, Aiden."

He slides a finger inside me, and the stretch from the single digit is mind-numbing. My ankles hook around his body, tugging him closer. There are no words sufficient for the pleasure pulsing through me. Before I can form a coherent thought, his tongue finds my clit, starting a slow, languid circle. "Fucking delicious."

It's... *Good* isn't close. Good is a weak adjective to describe how *out of this world* it all feels. Aiden takes his time, learning the combination of flicks of his tongue and curl of his finger that drives me wild. The rhythm that has me chanting his name again and again, sweat rolling between my breasts and my eyes fluttering closed. When I don't think I can take it anymore, so close to the edge, he adds a second finger, stretching me more, and more, *and more.*

I cry out and lift off the marble. It's almost too much. It's almost painful. I almost ask him to stop, but Aiden pauses, letting me adjust. He rubs my stomach with his left hand, a gentle pressure on my tense muscles. He kisses my thighs and my calves as he starts again, renewed vigor in his strokes.

"Feeling you clench around me is my new favorite thing in the world," he grinds out, teeth sinking into the soft part of my skin near my hip. "Need you around my cock."

"So fuck me," I gasp, threading my hands through his hair.

"Not until you come. Fuck, I want to taste it."

This raw, passionate side of him is disorienting. So is the way he bends over my body on the counter, eyes locked on mine as a third finger pushes inside. He kisses me through the pain and the fullness I feel deep in my stomach. He soothes me through the tears that spring to my eyes, and the gasp that works its way up my throat.

"I can't—"

"You can, sweetheart," he murmurs, kissing my jaw. "Prop up on your elbows so you can see how well you take me. Christ, Maggie, your pussy is swallowing my fingers."

I listen to him, adjusting my position so I can watch while he works me to the precipice of ecstasy. My thighs are wet, stained with arousal. His fingers are drenched, sliding in and out of me with ease, like we've been doing this for years. Slick sounds fill the air and combine with our heavy breathing. The front of Aiden's sweatpants are tight. The bulge of his erection tells me he's enjoying this as much as I am, and I haven't touched him yet. Then, he drops to his knees, kneeling, *bowing* before me, and his tongue is on me again, quick flicks working against my swollen clit.

"Yes," I hiss. "Right there. Don't stop, Aiden. I'm going to come."

I'm about to close my eyes, about to loll my head back and get swept away by his attention to detail, the way he already has my preferences figured out, the slow climb up the mountain and the peak I'm so close to reaching, when my gaze locks on a man in the building across from us. He's watching me. He's watching Aiden torture me to within an inch of my life. He's... *fuck*, he's not looking away. He *likes* it.

And I lose it. I explode in a flurry of stars and light, my orgasm reaching all the way from my head to my toes. Aiden doesn't stop, lapping up every drop of my release greedily as my legs shake and my body trembles.

I think years pass until I start to relax. I take a breath and my heart rate begins to slow, returning to normal. I wipe the back of my hand across my forehead to get rid of the sweat near my hairline.

"Wow," I finally whisper. His tongue slows and his fingers still. I peel myself off the counter and Aiden stands. His beard is damp. His eyes are dark. He steps toward me, cradling my face with a softer intensity than before. He brings his lips to mine, kissing me. I taste myself on his tongue, and it's the most wickedly delicious thing I've ever experienced in my life.

"What did I tell you?" Aiden growls. "A goddamn prize."

"That was... *five years*, Aiden? There's no way."

He laughs, rubbing his hand down my arm. "Feel less nervous?"

"Yeah," I say. "I also feel like I've died and gone to heaven. The best of both worlds." My limbs are heavy and my head is a little woozy, lust-drunk and sated. I'm pleased, *so* pleased, but I want more.

"And to think, the night is still young." He kisses me again before scooping me up. I peel off his shirt as he walks us down the hall and nearly run us into a wall.

"Now what?" I ask, draping my arms around his neck. His skin is warm, flushed with satisfaction, and I drag my fingernails down his chest.

"Now you're going to suck my cock like the good girl you are."

NINETEEN

MAGGIE

AIDEN DEPOSITS me at the entrance to his room. He stalks toward the bed, pulling off his sweatpants and boxer briefs. I watch the muscles of his bare ass flex and constrict with each step he takes. When he reaches the mattress, he stops and turns around.

I see him in his full form. Naked. Beautiful. *Hard*. I appreciate the length of his cock. Well above average, with some girth. Thick and wide without being a size that would have me terrified. He'll fit—just barely. I'm about to say something sexy, about how I can't wait to have him inside me, when I spot something on his leg, on the upper part of his left thigh.

"Is that the infamous tattoo?"

He grins and plops on the bed. "Yeah."

"What the hell is it?"

"A sun wearing sunglasses."

"Oh, my god. That's..."

"Stupid as hell, I know."

"But also kind of cool. It's like a metaphor. The sun is so bright, even he needs shades."

Aiden tips his head back and laughs. His shoulders shake,

and the sound is so lovely and pleasant. "God, I like you. You're so fun. Thanks for not ridiculing me."

My lips split into a wide grin. "I like you, too."

We stare at each other from across the room, and hilarity shifts to heated. Aiden spreads his legs and he grips his cock, lazily stroking the length up and down. "Take off your clothes, Maggie."

There's something about the way he looks at me that makes me feel sexy in a way I never thought I was before. It's like an aphrodisiac, a power radiating through me the longer he stares. I slide the sleeves of my dress down, and the material pools at my feet.

I unclasp my bra, freeing my breasts from the lace. Aiden's stoic facade wavers. His throat bobs, and I hear a strangled sound. My fingers hook in the waistband of my underwear, sliding them over my thighs and calves until I'm totally naked in front of him. His eyes roam down my body, from my neck to my toes, taking his time with a thorough perusal.

"By day, you're Maggie Houston. An extraordinary woman with a remarkable brain. Talented, nice as hell, and someone who puts others first. But tonight? Tonight, you're going to be the filthy fucking girl who's going to suck my cock, aren't you? The one who's going to let me fuck her from behind so I can appreciate her ass while I take care of her pussy. And you're going to say *thank you* every time. Now, get on your knees. Might as well get comfortable."

It's impossible to stop the moan hanging in my throat. It falls out, filling the room. I drop to the floor, my legs parting and my knees rubbing against the carpet. Need spreads down my spine like gasoline.

"I asked you a question," Aiden says. The sultry tone is gone, replaced with a firm command. My neck snaps up to meet his gaze, the once hazel eyes nearly obsidian with desire. Goosebumps sprout on my arms even though the temperature around me is scorching.

"Yes," I whisper. My throat is as dry and scratchy as sandpaper. "I am."

How can he be so in tune with my thoughts after reading a quick list? How can he know exactly what I'm looking for—what I've *craved* for years and finally allowed myself to voice, unabashedly acknowledging the things I so badly want to try?

He grins, a wicked smile stretching from either corner of his mouth. It's so different from the kind, friendly ones from earlier. This is a man in charge, one I'd hand the keys over to willingly.

He's going to wreck me, and I can't wait.

"Good. Now crawl over here, sweetheart, so I can paint your throat with my cum. I've been dreaming about your lips around my cock since the first time you said my name."

Degradation? *Check.* Full permission to use it going forward. My palms connect with the ground, and I start toward him. The shag of the carpet is welcomed, heightening my senses and making the journey far from humiliating. It's invigorating.

Aiden watches my every move. He strokes himself quicker, using jerkier movements. When I reach his parted thighs, slotting between them, his hand drops to my cheek.

"Good job, Maggie. I'm so proud of you."

I beam at the praise and rise up on my knees. "Thank you."

His fingers run through my hair and gently guide me to his cock. My mouth opens, taking just the head first. Salty pre-cum coats my tongue, and I lick it up greedily. I've given exactly six blow jobs in my life, all when I was in my early twenties, but I've listened to enough of Lacey's Tinder hookup stories to remember the mechanics.

"Don't rush," Aiden says. His grip tightens, pulling on my scalp. "I'm not in a hurry. I want this to feel good for you, too."

I nod and hollow out my cheeks, bringing him deeper in my

mouth. My tongue runs up the vein on the side of his length, and the groan I'm awarded tells me I've done the right thing. My right hand falls to the base of his shaft, joining the bob of my head to work in tandem.

I'm sloppy at first, trying to find a rhythm without hitting myself in the chin. After a few minutes it becomes easier, more familiar. I adjust my angle to see how far I can get him down my throat.

"There you go. Fucking perfect, Maggie. Are you wet right now?"

I pull off him with a *pop,* drool hanging in the corner of my mouth. Aiden reaches forward and wipes it away with his thumb, a proud glint in his eye. "I'm drenched."

"Sucking me off turns you on?"

I nod, torn on if I want to bring my fingers to my clit or to wrap them around his cock again. "I like seeing you..."

"Tell me," he says hoarsely. "Please."

"Powerless. Like I'm in control."

"You *are* in control. Whatever you say, goes. I'm fucking gone for you, and the only thing on my mind is making sure you enjoy tonight. We've got to be honest with each other, yeah?"

"Yeah," I agree. "We do."

"So touch yourself like I know you want to, and get your mouth back on me. I want you to take every inch of my cock."

I spring into action, my right hand slipping between my legs, my left making a fist and stroking him again. He encourages me with his soft moans. The whispers of, *yes, Maggie. So fucking good.* His palm at the nape of my neck, fingers close to curling around my windpipe. I undo him slowly, the way he undid me on the counter, bringing him close as I chase my own high.

"Aiden," I say, licking his shaft from the base to the tip. I cup his balls and he bucks his hips forward. "I want you to finish in my mouth."

"Are you close?" he grunts out. "I can't last much longer. Not when you're swirling your tongue like a menacing goddess."

"Yeah." I rub my clit in a circle. "I'm close."

"You first. You finish first, Maggie. Always."

The selflessness, the look in his eyes as he watches me with awe, and the feel of his weight in my hand sends me over the edge again. It's not as long lasting as the first orgasm, but it's *enough*.

Aiden tugs on my hair, bringing my lips back to his length. With a deep breath, I take him all the way into my mouth so he hits the back of my throat. He lets out a moan and I taste him, the salty, sticky sign of a man ravished and thoroughly satisfied sitting on my tongue, a flavor I've forgotten and missed.

"Fuck," he pants. He tilts my chin back carefully, scanning my face. "Are you okay?"

I take a second to answer, swallowing before I smile and lean forward to kiss him. "Never better."

"I think you're forgetting something."

My cheeks flame and I bite my lip. "Thank you, Aiden."

"Atta girl."

TWENTY

AIDEN

I'M TREADING A VERY slippery slope here.

The more time I spend with Maggie, the less I want her to leave. It's not just because she just gave me the best blow job of my life, either. It's because she feels *right* here. In the kitchen, over a bowl of pasta. In my bedroom, on her knees, looking up at me with glazed-over eyes and waiting for more. I just finished, but I feel invincible, like a man who's unbeatable and not someone who's forty-five. I think I could go for hours, the sounds of Maggie's moans spurring me on.

"Get on the bed," I say. I've never been one to care about being in charge, preferring to both lead *and* follow, but as I watch her climb on the mattress and crawl across the duvet, I think I like the idea of being the one calling the shots.

She stays on all fours, and it's the first time I get a good look at her ass. It's a glorious thing, round and pert with spankable cheeks, and I want to bite the smooth plane of pale skin. I walk to the bed and move behind her. Gently, I push on her lower back so her chest drops to the sheets. Her ass lifts in the air, an offering to me.

"Spread your legs wider. I want to see every inch of you,

Maggie. There you go," I say through an exhale as she does as I ask. "That's my fucking girl."

She moans at the praise, knees nearly buckling as she adjusts herself to a more open position. I trace down her spine, over each vertebrae, taking my time to learn her. I give her ass a squeeze and pinch one of her nipples.

"Look at this pretty pussy waiting for me. Christ, you're practically dripping."

"Dripping for you, Aiden," she answers, and I almost blow a load right there at her unfiltered admission. "I need you to fuck me. Please."

Please.

Every single time she says that word, I want to give her exactly what she wants, and more. If she wants me to fuck her, then I'm going to *fuck her*, so she'll never forget the first guy who ate her out. The first guy to run his finger between her ass cheeks as she comes on my cock, a tease of something else she might want to add to her list one day. The man who's going to rock her world and leave her sore, unable to walk straight for days.

I fumble with the condoms I laid out on the nightstand. I grab one and rip the wrapper open with unsteady hands. I work it down my length and press a kiss to her shoulder blade.

"I want you to touch your clit while I sink into you for the first time," I say. I grab a fistful of her hair to tilt her neck back, and Maggie lets out a gasp. "And don't forget your magic words."

She nods, a quick jerk of her head, and I watch her hand disappear between her legs. "Thank you, Aiden."

"Anything for you, sweetheart."

I line up at her entrance, taking a deep breath to school myself. *Fuck*, I'm nervous. I don't know why. I've done this before. Hundreds of times. Remembering how Maggie's ex never or satisfied her awakens a competitive beast inside of me. I want this to be perfect for her, because she deserves it.

I tease her at first, using my head to run through her slit. She's so *wet*. I know I'm not going to last long when I'm buried inside of her and feel how tight she is. I rock my hips forward half a degree, and suddenly I'm in her. Maggie cries out, nearly tumbling forward. I loop my arm around her middle to keep her upright, and kiss her neck.

"I got you," I murmur. "I promise."

It takes a minute for us both to get acclimated. I move in half an inch, then pause. Half an inch, then pause. It's exquisite, so warm and tight, and soon I'm one thrust away from being fully seated. We fit together perfectly.

"Aiden," she groans. "Move. I need to feel you."

"You can't feel me?" I withdraw out of her before slamming my hips forward. Maggie groans again, her left hand gripping the headboard. "What about now?" I thrust again, getting deeper than before.

"Yes." She gasps. "I feel you. And it feels so fucking good."

"That's what I thought. Hold on and don't let go."

Her filthy mouth encourages me. I alternate between a smack on her ass and a rock of my hips. And another, and another, and another. My assertiveness grows. Every time I pull out, I gawk at her arousal coating the condom. The circle of her wrist as she works herself to the edge. The hair spilling down her back like a waterfall and the sweat on her forehead.

"Are you going to come, Maggie?"

"I'm so full, Aiden. So full." She says it in gasps, her ass lifting higher and higher as she loses control. I reach around and pinch both her nipples between my thumb and pointer finger, feeling the overwhelming urge to touch her everywhere.

"If you were mine," I say into the crook of her neck, "I wouldn't need to wear a condom. Your ass would look fucking divine covered in my cum. Even better, dripping from your pussy, so everyone knew who made you feel so fucking good."

I can tell the moment she comes. She lets out the loudest moan yet, clenching and fluttering around my dick like it's giving her pussy life. She takes control of the tempo, rocking back into me and wiggling her hips, a circle motion that makes my eyes roll.

I lose it, then. It's all too much. It's all too fan-fucking-tastic. All I can offer is three more short, staccato movements before I collapse over her, my sweat-soaked chest colliding with her back. With as much energy as I can muster, I drop my head to her shoulder and gulp down air.

"You good?" I ask, wanting to make sure she's alright. Maggie doesn't answer right away. I wince as I pull out of her, and I see tears in her eyes. "Hey, sweetheart. Talk to me. Did I hurt you?"

"No." She shakes her head violently. "It was so good. I don't know why I'm crying when I enjoyed every second."

"Admit it. I rocked your world."

"Glad to see you're humble." She gives me a watery smile. "Sorry, I'm making this so weird."

"You're not making it weird." I get rid of the condom, tying it and tossing it in the wastebasket by my bed. "Sex is emotional, even if you take the emotions out of it. C'mere."

I lay on my side, opening my arms so Maggie can make her way into my embrace. She curls up, her back to my front, and her hands fold across mine. "Thank you."

"For what?"

"For the mind-blowing orgasms. For being so kind. For... I don't know. Suggesting a one-night stand in the first place and getting me out of my sex-less slump."

"Thank you for coming over. I'm happy I could help." I run my hand down her arm and she shivers. "Cold?"

"A little."

"Lift up." With some maneuvering, we make our way under the covers, and Maggie relaxes, molding her body into mine. "I wasn't too aggressive, was I?"

The shake of her head is quick. "No, you weren't." She spins and buries her face in my chest. "Please keep talking like that."

"Embarrassed, huh?" I chuckle, running my fingers through her hair. I work out a particularly knotted strand.

"No. It's just, you're such a nice guy outside the bedroom, then you go and have a filthy mouth. It's perfect. The exact balance I wondered if I would actually like. Turns out, I do. A lot."

"Add it to your list. Are you tired?"

"Physically? Sort of. But I don't want to go to sleep. Not when I have so few hours with you."

She glances up at me, and I smile at the smeared lipstick and bite marks on her neck. She looks thoroughly fucked, courtesy of me, and I'm a proud bastard at the sight of her.

"What are you thinking about?" she asks.

"You. It's a shame we both don't want a relationship, because I could fuck you every night. But, more importantly, I'm hoping you're okay."

"I'm good." She kisses my chin. "I promise."

TWENTY-ONE
MAGGIE

I AM GOOD. I don't think I've ever felt so... complete. It's a weird word to use after sex, but it seems the most appropriate. There was physical pleasure, yes. My back arching, Aiden's fingers pinching. His grunts and my moans. A high I've never soared to before, and one I'm eager to ascend again. But there was extreme tenderness, too, from him, in a time where there didn't need to be. Patience and certainty of making things *right* for me.

His arms are sturdy, wrapped around my body in a considerate hold. My fingers run from his wrists to his bicep, marking a path on his skin. Here, in an unfamiliar bed, with a man I've just met, the spin of the fan whirring above, I've never felt so valued or cared for. The moments of intensity have simmered, cooling to a collective calm where everything feels *right*.

Aiden's eyes close, long eyelashes fanning out over his cheeks. Our breathing syncs, leveling out to a restful hum. I reach up and brush a lock of hair off his forehead, smiling at the gray I find.

"Tell me a secret," I say softly.

He hums and draws me closer, my cheek resting on his chest. "What kind of secret?"

"I don't know. Something personal."

"I thought we were avoiding talking about personal things?" he counters. His eyes open, and a playful gleam winks back at me.

"We are. But I need a second to breathe, and I like listening to you talk."

Aiden's chuckle is deep, a sound pulled from within his soul. My palm traverses from his shoulder to his heart, the organ beating rhythmically against my hand. "Maven's mom cheated on me. That's why we got divorced."

"What?" I sit up on my elbow, staring down at him. "Are you serious?"

"Yeah, but I promise it's not as bad as it sounds. Katie, my ex, was spending a lot of time with a woman from work. It was all innocent, of course. Shopping on the weekend. Wine nights during the week. One day, she came home and told me they kissed. It wasn't premeditated, but a heat of the moment kind of thing. Their eyes locked, and they just knew. Katie felt so guilty, and she told me that when it happened, everything made sense. She said it had never been like that with me. This part of her she had denied existed for years finally came to the surface. She had always been attracted to women and was too afraid to say anything. We were happy, sure, but her and Naomi? Those two are endgame."

"You don't sound upset."

"Right after, I was hurt. I started therapy and reflected on any signs I might have missed. It was selfish to insert myself into the narrative, when it wasn't about me. Katie loved me, but she loves that part of herself more. As she should. How could I ever be mad at someone who gets to live so authentically now? She found true love, with no secrets, just herself. Isn't that what we're all searching for anyway?"

"Those are profound words from someone who doesn't want

a relationship."

"I don't want a relationship because of logistics. But I'm still a human. I crave physical and emotional connections like everyone else."

"Do you think we're all lucky enough to find that love? The soul-crushing, can't eat, can't sleep kind of infatuation?"

Aiden pauses before answering. He tucks a piece of hair behind my ear. His thumb strokes across my cheek. "No. That love is rare. Sometimes even the ones in it don't realize how lucky they are. It's a tough pill to swallow, but I have hope. And hope is half the battle, isn't it?"

His words strike a chord with me. I was in a loveless marriage for years. Millions of other people are, too. There are famous lines about not knowing what you have until it's gone, and the devastating realization about finding out what you lost.

Despite the heartbreak I've suffered, the cynical whisperings that rear their ugly heads in moments of weakness or loneliness, there is a wisp of hope left. A small yet mighty pounding in my ears assuring me it might not happen tomorrow, or next week, or even next year. But one day, I *will* have that love again. And when I do, I'm never going to let it go.

"I came here for sex," I whisper. "And you hit me with philosophical deepness."

"When you hit forty, you turn all introspective. You've got a few years to go." He grins at me. "Sorry for all the real talk. I'll make up for it with my fingers in a few minutes."

"Don't apologize. Thank you for sharing your heart with me, Aiden Wood."

"I've been lonely for almost five years. Then, on a whim, I walk into a warehouse and meet you. I don't know what that means in the grand scheme of life, but it's got to be worth something, if only for a little while. Being here with you tonight renews that hope I have."

"Yeah." I lean forward. My mouth hovers above his. "It does mean something."

The conversation dies. His hand twists in my hair and his lips cover mine. With an agile move, Aiden flips us, switching our positions. My head rests against the pillow as he centers himself between my legs.

"I like looking at you," he says, pulling away. He sits back on his heels. "I want to watch you touch yourself."

"Sick of touching me already?" I joke.

Aiden's jaw ticks. "I could touch you for the rest of my life and it would never be enough, Maggie," he answers. It lodges in my chest like a venomous arrow, and I know he's being honest. There's not an ounce of humor in those words, and this is the first time since I've walked into his apartment where I wonder if I've made a grave mistake. Not out of regret, but because of how fucking *difficult* it's going to be to walk away.

"You did just fine out in the kitchen."

"Ah, yes. Every man strives to hear he did *fine*." I swat at him, and he pins my arms above my head. "I want you to show me what you like," he continues. "What makes you feel good? What are you going to think about at night when my mouth isn't on your pussy?"

Sweat beads on my forehead and I take a shallow breath. I've never masturbated in front of anyone before, and it's thrilling to know he wants to learn how I lift my hips. The pattern of my fingers and how many I use. The angle of my legs and how deep I can get.

"Are you going to film it?" I ask, wiggling my butt on the sheets and sitting up.

Aiden's eyes darken. His hands drop from my wrists and his fingers curl around my chin. "Don't tempt me with a good time. Maybe I will record you. I'd use it after you left, my hand jerking my dick to the sound of your moans and your wet, sweet pussy.

Then maybe, if I was drunk and missing you, five shots deep in a bottle of whiskey, I'd be reckless and send the video to you. I'd ask if you still curl your toes or throw your head back, and wonder if you found someone who knew what they were doing. I'd tell you how my sheets still smell like your cum and I can still taste you on my tongue. And then I'd ask if you missed me, too."

The words almost send me spiraling over the edge. My face heats and my nipples harden. I'm staining the sheets, I know I am, but I can't find it in myself to care. This man wants me, and I think he might die without me.

"Okay Doctor Wood," I say quietly. Aiden grunts, and his hand drops to his cock, tugging himself once. "You're so close to begging. Maybe you should get on your knees."

"You want me on my knees? I'd do it willingly. I would beg for you, Maggie. And plead, too, if that's what it took. But don't be too smug. It's my cock that made you come earlier, and I'm going to do it again."

"It's hard to touch myself when you're straddling my legs," I point out. Aiden grins and drops a kiss to my forehead. It's his favorite spot, I've learned.

"Forgive me for not wanting to pull away from you, for even a second." He climbs off me and takes up space at the end of the bed. His hand covers his cock and he waits patiently, eyes trained on mine.

I take a deep breath and slink down on the pillows, my back flush against the mattress. I close my eyes and run my hand down my chest. I palm my breast and play with my nipple, a sigh escaping my mouth.

"You like touching your tits," Aiden says. It sounds like it's through clenched teeth, grinding his molars together.

"I don't know why people skip them." I move to the other side, back rising off the bed as I pinch this nipple with more pressure. "It feels so good."

If I were alone, I'd spend more time on my chest. With an audience, though, I want to keep the show going. My hand slides down my stomach, and I open my legs.

"I know some women love to fuck themselves with their fingers, but I love to play with my clit." I don't know how I'm able to say these things, a salacious side of myself I never knew existed. It's freeing to put this in the world, to own the things I like. Why should I be embarrassed enjoying what gets me off?

I don't have to open my eyes to know Aiden's moving closer. The mattress shifts, and I feel the heat of his body engulfing mine. I hear the huff of his breath and the drawn out *fuck* he whispers when I circle my clit in slow strokes.

"I like to take my time," I say. "It's when I think about the things I want to try. I imagine myself in the books."

"Open up, baby. Let me see how wet you get when you fantasize about your wildest dreams. Tell me about them"

My thighs part. My tongue is loose and my mind is exploding with a thousand images. "Sometimes I imagine two guys taking me at once. Sometimes I imagine being fucked in a public place. Sometimes I imagine my ass red and covered with marks from someone's hand. And sometimes, I pretend I'm being held by someone who loves and respects me so deeply, while also knowing exactly what I need."

"Jesus," he groans. I slide a finger inside myself, still stretched from Aiden, still wet from my last orgasm, and let out a moan. "Maggie."

"And when I go home tomorrow, I'll think of this. You'll be what I imagine as I tease myself over my underwear. When I go from one finger to two, prepping for a toy that won't come close to how good your cock feels inside me. I'll think about you, Aiden, when I'm sober as hell, wondering if you're thinking about me, too."

I circle my clit four times, that feeling rising in my belly. I'm close to capturing it, close to giving in, when a hand curls around my wrist, stopping me.

"Get on your knees," Aiden growls.

I grin, my eyes opening slowly, no remorse for the high I've yet to reach. "So much for self-control."

"Fuck self-control."

It happens so fast. I spin. He rips open a condom. My fingers curl around the sheets, waiting, *dying* for him. And then he's inside me again, claiming every inch of me.

"You take me so well," he says, voice singed with pride.

His grip tightens on my hips, fingers pushing into the pulse point of my skin that burns like a wildfire at the apex of my thigh. Maybe I should get a tattoo of his fingerprint, the outline of his thumb so I'll have this feeling forever embedded, a permanent fixture, because nothing has ever felt so good.

"It's like you were made for my cock. No one else's. Mine and mine alone."

"Yours, Aiden," I agree. It's the truth. After tonight, I'll be ruined. He'll be known as The Best Ever. The One Who Got Away. No one will ever be able to top Aiden Wood.

His hips meet mine with chaotic thrusts. It's rough, messy, and *perfect*. Even better than the first time. His hand connects with my ass. My nails dig into his thighs. He yanks my hair. I call out his name. It's a choreographed routine we've already memorized. He squeezes my backside, and I know he's close to finishing.

"You first," he says with that familiar selflessness. Before I can snake my hand between my legs, his fingers are there, circling and rubbing and pushing me over the edge. I tumble gladly, the free-fall well worth the climb, and I collapse into an exhausted heap on the mattress.

"Come in me, Aiden," I say through tired breaths, reaching back to touch him anywhere my hands can find.

And he does. Through a long groan and two more rocks forward, I feel his release. He pumps in me until he finally stills, stilted pants gasping for air filling the room.

"I think I'm dying," he says. "Dead at forty-five thanks to the way you ride my dick."

I burst out laughing and ease myself off him. "I'll mourn you."

"Show up naked to my funeral so I can appreciate your ass one more time."

"I think that can be arranged."

We climb over each other and shuffle around on the bed, finding our way back to the position we started in. Me, in his arms. Him, a kiss to my forehead.

"I'm going to need multiple hours of recovery," he admits. "I haven't gone this many times since... fuck. Ever, I think."

"And they say men get progressively worse with age. I have some data to submit."

"Let me make sure I don't go into cardiac arrest first. Are you okay if we put a brief pause on physical activities? Then you can continue to research."

"Aiden. We could go the rest of our time together without having sex again, and it'd still be the best night of my life."

"Good. I want to just... be with you."

"And what does that entail?" I ask, snuggling into him.

"Some quiet for a few minutes. A shower when my legs can move properly. Talking. Making a second dinner. I don't care. Just want to enjoy you." He buries his face in my hair and sighs. "Ten hours with you, and you're already one of my favorite people. Scary, isn't it?"

"Yeah," I whisper. I close my eyes and take a deep breath. There's sweat on my back. My hair is a mess. I need to use the bathroom, and my calf is cramping. Still, there's nowhere I'd rather be. Nothing has ever felt more like home. "Terrifying."

TWENTY-TWO
AIDEN

WE LIE TOGETHER FOR AN HOUR. We'll talk occasionally. She shares a story about her family. I mention the secret signed *Lord of the Rings* movie poster I have in my closet, and how I'd grab it if there was a fire. For the most part, we're quiet, holding each other and reveling in the silence. There's no urgency to speak. It's still and peaceful and fucking *perfect*.

Eventually, Maggie drags me into the bathroom to shower. I turn on the water and she shrieks about it being too cold. Something lethal in my chest twists and turns as she splashes me with droplets, elated laughter ringing in my ears. The longer I stare at her—naked, a nasty bruise sprouting on her neck from where I sucked her skin, tousled hair and a smile on her face—the more painful the sensation is.

It hits me suddenly.

I don't want her to leave. I want her to stay here. Not just for tonight, but for many nights after. I imagine a toothbrush next to mine and her scrubs in my hamper. Hair ties on the vanity and scented soap on her side of the sink.

Instead of being an adult who has open conversations,

instead of proposing a real date rather than something confined strictly to the walls of my apartment with an expiration date, I keep my mouth closed and nudge her in the shower. It accommodates two people well, and there's plenty of space to sink to my knees, water trickling down my chest as I prop Maggie's leg on my shoulder. I tell her to put her hands above her head, to keep her eyes on me, and then I eat her out because it's easier than saying I could see her fitting into my life.

I bring her to the brink and stop just short of finishing her off. Multiple times. One minute, she curses me and calls me an asshole. In the next, as her toes curl over my muscles and she lets out a sob of desperation, she calls me God, a hymn I want to hear every day.

Her balance is shaky. Her thighs quake. Still, she behaves. Her hands stay in place, her eyes stay open, and she's listening so well, being so *good,* I know she deserves to be rewarded. I ask her to pass me the detachable shower head. I bring it to her clit, holding her steady as she comes—twice, because, fuck me, she's perfect. She whispers *thank you* so beautifully, and I want to get the words tattooed on me so I can remember them forever.

I stop the water and grab a towel, drying her off. I take my time, massaging her muscles, running down the length of her body, appreciating every divot, every dip, every curve. I kiss her dry skin as I go, savoring the heat under my lips.

In a fit of selfishness, I steal one more orgasm from her as I run the terry cloth between her legs. It doesn't take much, hardly a graze over her clit and the slip of my finger inside, until she's coming again, juices from her pussy running down my hand.

I gather her in my arms and bring her back to bed, the discussion of a potential second meeting shoved away, locked in a compartment I can't open, because this arrangement is what we want. I refuse to jeopardize what we have going with a silly declaration of feelings, no matter how poignant they might feel.

I haven't bounced back yet physically, dick still soft and spent, so I tie Maggie's hands together with one of my patterned neck accessories. I cover her eyes with an eye mask I have in my dresser from an overnight flight a couple years back. I tease her, touching every inch of her body until I know exactly what she likes and where. She gets frustrated with me for being so slow and thorough. Her wrists yank against the tie, the skin under the silk turning pink. I flip her on her knees and spank her for rushing me, another check off her list.

After I make her come, I can tell she's depleted. I hold her close, stroking her damp hair and listening to her talk about how she got into neurosurgery.

"Did you want to be a doctor growing up?"

"No." She laughs. Her hand draws lazy circles on my arm. "I wanted to be a receptionist in a doctor's office. I would set up a fake desk with a keyboard and type, pretending I was looking up patient information."

"What made you pursue the medical field, then?"

"A kid in middle school said girls weren't as smart as boys. He told me girls should be teachers, because it's easy, and only boys get to do the hard jobs. As if teaching is easy. My sister is in education, and you couldn't pay me to put up with the shit she does. Teachers are miracle workers."

"My brother is in education, too. You're right. Their profession is wrongfully shit on. I wouldn't last a day in a classroom. Did you ever track the douchebag down and tell him about your success?"

"I did one better. I sent him an invitation to my med school graduation. And when the news article came out about me accepting my current role, I forwarded it to him on Facebook."

"Maggie Houston." I laugh. "You're a badass."

"More like petty and bitter, but I'll accept the compliment." She pauses. "Would you tell me more about Maven?"

"Of course. What do you want to know?"

"Anything you're willing to share."

I smile on instinct thinking about her. "She wasn't planned. I wasn't sure if I even wanted kids, to be honest. The day she was born, though, I fell hopelessly in love. I realized I was put on this earth to be her dad. No title after my name will ever be as good as that."

"Do you two get along?"

"Yeah. It's hard to find the boundary between parent and friend sometimes. I'll do a stupid TikTok dance with her, but then I have to scold her for not finishing her homework. It's a give and take. Sixteen years, and I'm still learning. I'm far from a perfect father, but I do my best."

"That's all we can ask for from our parents. You love her, and you show her you love her. The rest is just extra." Maggie sighs. "You're lucky."

I hear the remorse in her tone. I know there's a story there, a part of her life she's keeping tucked away, sheltered from scrutiny. Understanding the heaviness settling between us, I rub Maggie's shoulder. "I am. But kids don't define a person."

"I got divorced because I couldn't have children," she says. It's so soft, so broken, I can't help but bring her closer and squeeze her tight.

"Sweetheart, I don't want you to feel obligated to share anything personal with me just because I did. You're allowed to keep parts of yourself private."

"I want to tell you, though. Unless you don't want to hear it."

"Maggie," I say. "I want to hear everything you have to say. I promise to listen. And if you start a story and decide halfway through you don't want to talk anymore, that's okay, too."

She nods and gnaws on her bottom lip. I wait, letting her take the time she needs.

"My ex and I got married after a few years together, and we were on the same page about wanting children. We started trying right after the wedding. It's rare that it happens so soon, so we were patient. My in-laws began pressuring us. My friends were having kids, and we weren't. We tried, and nothing worked. A couple years passed, and after multiple visits with specialists, I was told I'm unable to have children. And that was it. My marriage fell apart afterward. We got divorced. I'll always have that hole in my heart, I think, of wanting something and not being able to have it."

I hear her sniff, and a fitful burst of protection barrels into me. I need to comfort her. I need to wipe away her tears. I need her to know how wonderful she is.

"Sweetheart," I whisper. I peel myself out from under her, and sit up. She's beautiful under the light of the moon. "There are other paths you could take. Have you looked into adoption?"

"I work sixty hours a week. It'd be impossible to raise a child on my own. I'm making this a big deal. I'm fine, I promise. Therapy helps a lot. I have nieces and nephews who I love. Maybe one day, when I find the man I'll marry, he'll have a family from a previous life, and I'll fit in with them."

"Found family is still family. Just because it's not blood doesn't mean it's less special."

"I know. It's like you said earlier. We have to have hope, right?"

"Right," I say. "Thank you for sharing with me. You're an incredible woman, Maggie, and I'm sorry anyone has ever made you feel less than wonderful."

"One day, someone's going to scoop you up, Aiden," she says softly. I see a flicker in her eye, the brightness dimming. "And they're going to be very lucky."

"The same goes for you. Promise me you'll never settle for less than someone who treats you like the queen you are."

Maggie leans forward. She climbs into my lap, straddling my thighs. Her lips press to my hairline, and her hand cups the scruff of my beard. "I promise."

I'm the biggest idiot known to man.

God dammit.

TWENTY-THREE
MAGGIE

"WHAT TIME IS IT?" I ask Aiden.

I hear him fumble with his phone, the screen bright in the darkened room. We haven't turned on the lamp on his nightstand, content to enjoy each other under the moonbeams without the harshness of artificial lighting.

"Ten," he answers. "Are you doing okay?"

"Yeah." My stomach picks that moment to grumble. I wince and cover my belly with my hand. "Sorry."

"Sounds like you're hungry."

"I've been put through a cardio boot camp. You've also made me come, like, nine times. I could eat. Do you want me to head out?"

Aiden furrows his brows. "What? Why would I want you to do that?"

"I don't know. We had sex. This could be the route you take to send me on my way."

He positions himself above me, staring me in the eyes. "Just because you're hungry? You said I got you for twenty-four hours, Maggie. I intend to keep you until the very last second."

I wrap my arms around his neck. "I don't want to leave," I clarify.

God, no. I feel like I could make a home for myself in Aiden's place. Every second I stay here, it makes it seem more plausible. A dream turning into a reality. I'm glad he's not eager to kick me out, because I'm not through with him yet.

"Take your pick. Pizza delivered, or something homemade."

"You already cooked for me."

"I did, sweetheart, and I'm offering to make you something else."

I grin. "In that case, homemade."

"How does grilled cheese sound?"

"Like heaven."

Aiden kisses me softly. "Coming right up."

Ten minutes later we're in his kitchen. I'm wearing an old shirt of his, the logo of a sports team etched across my chest. The black cotton is long, and hangs to the top of my thighs. He pulled on another pair of gray sweatpants and is standing over the stove, humming as he flips the sandwiches.

I watch his muscles flex. I stare at the tufts of hair curling at the back of his neck, and the love handles at the hem of his pants. He's more attractive to me now, away from the lights of the shoot. He was confident through the whole session, but it's different to watch Aiden in real life. I'm learning little nuances about him; ones others might miss, but I'm actively searching for. To me, they're as plain as day.

Like how he flips each sandwich three times. The way he starts a task, pauses to complete something else entirely, then resumes his original chore. The methodical order of plates and cutlery on the countertop; placemat, plate, glass, fork.

"My lady," Aiden says, setting the finished sandwich on my plate.

"Thank you." I take a bite and moan around the melted cheese. "My god, Aiden. What did you put in this?"

"The secret is mayo on the bread before you cook it. It helps give it a little crunch." He sits next to me, and his knee nudges mine. "I'm kind of jealous grilled cheese got you to make that sound. I haven't heard it yet."

"Still plenty of time left." I grin and take another bite. "Have you ever broken a bone?"

"Nope. I did sprain my ankle when I was thirty, though, in some kickball fundraiser my best friend signed me up for. It's the last time I played competitive sports."

"I've heard about him. Football coach, right?"

"Yeah. Shawn. We've known each other for decades. He's Maven's godfather, actually."

"Is he single?"

"Why? Interested?" Aiden quirks his eyebrow.

"Definitely not my type. But he might be Lacey's type."

"Tell me about her. She's your best friend?"

"Yeah. We met in med school, and we've been friends ever since. We're a good pair of opposites that balance each other out."

"What kind of medicine does she practice?"

"She's a pediatrician, and she's incredibly kind. Selfless, too, and very good at her job."

"She sounds like you."

"You think I'm selfless?" I ask, and I take another bite.

"Wholeheartedly. You helped your friend out with something you weren't sure you were going to enjoy. You thanked the assistants on set who brought you coffee with a smile and treated them like equals. I might not know a whole lot about you, Maggie, but I can tell you're a person who puts others first."

"Speaking of selflessness, look at you. Handing out grilled cheeses to hungry folks. You're a good host."

Aiden licks his fingers clean and takes our empty plates to the sink. "Orgasms and food. Put me down in the record books as the best ever."

"There's that humbleness, again."

He laughs, rinsing the porcelain then coming back over to take my hand. He pulls me from the bar stool and wraps his arms around my waist. "You're a smart-ass."

"You called me selfless two minutes ago."

"Potato, potahto."

I rest my head on his shoulder and stare out at the twinkling city lights. "Aiden?"

"Hm?"

"Thank you for such a wonderful night. I wasn't sure what was going to happen when I came over here, but you've exceeded all of my expectations."

"Right back at you." He stands on his toes and kisses the top of my head. "I'm glad I did the shoot. It meant meeting you."

Those words are important, I know. Some cosmic arrangement of the universe so our paths would cross, destined to intertwine. In another life, maybe we could be something. A couple that spent quiet moments together after a long day of loud noises, unwinding on the couch, side by side. He'd make me tea. I'd help clean up. It would *work*, a match made in heaven.

"You're thinking hard," he murmurs.

"Sorry. Just daydreaming."

Aiden hums. "Do something for me?" he asks.

"Bend over the stool?"

"We'll do that soon, but not yet. Will you dance with me?"

"Here? In the kitchen? While I'm not wearing underwear?"

"Well, now I do want to bend you over the stool."

I nudge his chest. "You want to dance with me?"

"Yeah. I do." He spins me out of his hold and laces our fingers together. "We've done dinner and dessert. I bought you flowers. We had incredible sex. All that's left to make this a perfect date is some dancing. It is Valentine's Day, after all."

"I wasn't aware this was a date," I say softly. He tugs me and wraps his arms around my waist. We sway together, my back to his front, a synchronized movement. I hear Aiden hum a tune, *La Vie en Rose*, I think, and I close my eyes.

"It's not. I would've done everything different if this were an actual date. You mentioned liking roller blading. I would have suggested we meet at the Air and Space museum. Blade down the National Mall, then grab a burger for lunch. We'd sit on a bench, talk, and freeze our asses off. I'd probably spill ketchup on my shirt. You'd laugh at me for being a goof. I'd be scared shitless to ask you out again, but you'd take pity on me and agree."

"You'd rollerblade with me even though you hate athletics? And you could possibly tear a ligament?"

"Of course," he says simply. "You like it."

"Will we have candy hearts with our burgers?"

"All the candy hearts you want, sweetheart. An homage to our first meeting."

I could stay like this forever. In his hold, the press of his lips to my cheek, the hum of his voice as he dips me low to the ground, a brilliant smile on his face. It's a shame I'm going to have to say goodbye.

TWENTY-FOUR
AIDEN

"I THINK we should revisit a couple of items from your list." I pick up the forgotten piece of paper, reading over the items Maggie jotted down.

"Any personal favorites, Doctor Wood?" she asks.

"The crawling was hot as hell. And you on the counter was sexy, too."

"So you're a man who likes to be in control and wants to show me off to the world."

"I'd be an idiot to not want that, Maggie. You're a trophy."

Her cheeks flush. She loves to be praised, but accepting compliments at the drop of a hat isn't as easy. I only have a few more hours to prove to her that she *is* worthy of that praise, and more.

"Get on your knees," I say. I toss the paper to the side, not giving a flying fuck where it ends up. I have it all memorized. "And lose the shirt."

Maggie pulls the cotton over her head, naked body fully visible. She lowers herself to the floor, wincing as her knees connect with the laminate. Once situated, she looks up at me with inquisitive eyes, waiting for the next set of instructions. I stroke the top of her head and bend down to press a kiss to her knotted hair. She lets out a sigh, a sign she's okay, and I make my way to the window. Leaning against the glass, I tug my sweats below my ass, not bothering to take them off completely.

"Touch your nipples," I instruct. Her hands move automatically, palming her breasts and twisting her nipples between her fingers. Her neck tilts back and her throat elongates. "One hand on your clit. There you go, Maggie. Fucking perfect."

She lets out a breathy little moan, a tiny exhale of air. God, I want to touch her. To coax her over the edge myself, swallowing down every sound she tries to make. I stay mounted to the window, though, my eyes hooded and my dick as hard as a fucking rock.

Maggie rubs her clit with her right hand, and pinches her nipple with her left. She has a rhythm, a specific pace she enjoys, and I watch her, every circle of her finger. Every flick against a pebbled peak. I really would record her if I could. I'd play the video every night, zooming in so I could see the glisten of her fingers as she fucked herself into oblivion.

"Come over here, sweetheart. I want you to suck my cock." Maggie goes to stand and I tut. "Really? Think about your next move very carefully. If you choose incorrectly, you'll end up over my knee."

"And if I pick the right choice?"

"You'll suck my dick, then I'll fuck you against the window. And after, what will you say?"

I'm not a guy who narrates each move during intimacy, but I've always been a fan of saying exactly what's on my mind when it comes to sex. Why bother with games and ambiguity when I could have her flat on her back, legs wrapped around my neck? I was afraid the directness might be too much for Maggie, but she doesn't mind. Her inhale is sharp like jagged glass. Pink flushes her cheeks, and her rhythm on her clit becomes sporadic.

"Thank you," she whispers.

"Such a good girl."

The praise lights her up. She smiles and her eyes brighten. Her hands fall to her sides and she leans forward, palms flat against the floor.

Jesus. I've never made a woman crawl to me before, but *fuck* does Maggie make it look sexy as hell. Her gaze stays locked on mine as she makes her way to me. Left hand. Right hand. Left hand. Right hand.

"I think you like watching me crawl," she says. "On all fours, staring up at you."

"I don't just like it. I fucking love it. And don't bother being shy. I know you like it, too. You're probably dripping on my floor with how much you're enjoying yourself."

When she reaches me, she looks up, waiting. I nod once, and before I can blink, her mouth is on me, licking my dick like it's the last drops of water on earth. I groan and my head rests against the glass, eyes closing and welcoming how good the swirl of her tongue is. The pressure on my balls as she rubs them in her hand. I buck my hips forward when she deep throats me, and how the fuck I don't lose total control right then and there is a wonder.

She bobs her head, from the base of my shaft to the tip, moaning around my length. Her mouth is fucking fantastic, and her hands—those small, delicate hands—are little devils. I'm close, and if she keeps her lips around me for another minute, I'm going to be done for.

My fingers thread through her hair and tug, hard. She lets out a little gasp and releases me with a *pop.*

"Stop," I get out, voice hoarse. "Get up here so I can fuck you."

Maggie stands and I lift her into my arms. Her legs wrap

around my waist and I spin us so her back is against the windows. She hisses as the cold glass touches her skin.

"Aiden," she whispers. She rolls her hips into me, hands squeezing my shoulders.

"Get your hands above your head." When she complies, I dig into my pocket to grab the condom I put in there earlier. I rip the wrapper open with my teeth, holding her with one arm as I slide the latex over my shaft.

"You're so hot," she says.

"Say that again when I'm inside you." I slide my hands under her ass and sink her onto my dick in one swift motion. She groans, and her palms slide down the glass. "Drop your hands, and I'll make you stand in front of the window naked while I take you over my knee."

"Fuck," she moans. Her fingers latch onto the pane, holding herself steady.

Some thread of restraint snaps, and I fuck her with abandon. I'm rough, needy. It's been too long without her pussy on me, and I'm dying without it. She's going to have marks on her body tomorrow from my grip. I'm afraid if I let her go, she'll float away forever.

"You feel so good," I whisper into her ear. "Tell me, sweetheart, who's pussy is this?"

"Yours. Yours, Aiden."

It's music to my fucking ears, and possessiveness rolls through me. "That's my girl."

"You're so hot," she says again, and I have to bite back my laughter through a grunt because, *fuck*, she's perfect.

"God, Maggie. You're so fucking sexy. Shameless, too, taking my cock for the whole city to see. No one fills you like I do, do they? No one takes care of you like I do. No one makes you come like I do. And when you leave tomorrow, you're going to think of me buried in your tight pussy and wish you were still here."

"Yes," she cries out. I reach between us, my thumb finding her clit and rubbing.

"Come on my cock like the good girl you are, Maggie. Let me feel you clench around me."

An incoherent mess of sounds tumble out of her. Her eyes squeeze closed. Her back arches and I capture her nipple in my teeth. I think she stops breathing, going scarily silent until I feel her pussy flutter and she lets out the longest, loudest moan I've ever heard.

"Aiden," she sobs. "Thank you."

I don't give her time to catch her breath. I pull out of her and rip off the condom. I set her on her knees and yank her head back. "Suck, Maggie. I want you to swallow all of it."

Tears travel down her cheeks, but her lips part eagerly. She takes me in her mouth, closing around my shaft with hollowed-out cheeks. Maggie is like a drug, the kind that can ruin your life; one hit, I want to do it again. Two hits, I'm an addict.

It doesn't take much, and when she angles her head, fitting my whole length in her mouth, I don't stand a chance. I groan, painting her throat with my cum, just like I told her I would, for the second time tonight. Even after I finish, she continues to suck, taking every last drop I'm willing to give her.

"Maggie," I say. I stroke her hair gently, my muscles pliant and spent.

She releases me. When she looks up, my heart fractures. Her hair is a mess and there is drool on her chin. Still, she's the most beautiful woman I've ever seen. She presses a kiss to my thigh and stands on shaky legs to wrap her arms around my waist.

"Thank you," she says into my chest. "Best night ever."

TWENTY-FIVE
AIDEN

I DON'T KNOW what time it is. I know we haven't slept, just kind of floated between awake and asleep. I'll close my eyes for a moment too long, then Maggie will snuggle into me and kiss my shoulder. I'll be revitalized, snapping back to life. I'm exhausted, but I also feel so alive, like I could run for miles and miles and never grow tired.

I peer down at her, watching the soft breaths she takes. She's asleep, I think, curled around my waist. Her hair is sleep-mussed and a mess of tangles. Her lips are swollen and hickeys litter her neck. I smile as I drag my thumb over a bruise, appreciating the mark on her skin.

She's so physically stunning. An absolute knockout of a woman and a goddess walking amongst mortals. The radiance is hard to miss, the first thing you recognize about her. When you dig deeper, when you talk to her, you realize how brilliant she is, too. I'd fall on my knees to worship her beauty. Intellectually, though, she's my goddamn kryptonite. My Achilles' heel that would cause me to blunder my deepest secrets and darkest confessions at the snap of a finger.

She's quick, witty, and hands down the smartest person I've

talked to in decades. I wish I could sit with her for days, listening to the wonders of her brain and the depths of her knowledge. It's an alarmingly attractive, substantially important thing. I was a damn fool for thinking I could rid myself of her after only twenty-four hours together, because one night won't be enough.

Fuck. An entire lifetime probably wouldn't be enough.

I drop a kiss to the top of her head and hear her sigh. She's awake now, savoring the final moments of quiet contentment. Morning light trickles through the curtains to the left of the bed we've made our oasis. I hate the sight of sunlight. Sunlight means a new day. A day where she leaves, and that's that. It's a tragic thought, and she must be realizing it, too, because she stiffens against me.

"Morning," I say softly.

"Hey," she breathes out. She shifts her position to lie flat on her stomach, and she turns her head to smile at me. Her hand reaches out and she rests her palm against my beard. "Did you get any sleep?"

"No. I wasn't tired." I kiss her wrist, my lips pressing over the red left behind from the tie around her hands. "Are you hungry? I could make us pancakes."

"Not for food," she murmurs. "Not yet."

"My girl." I lift her into my arms and position her so she's in my lap, straddling my thighs. "My beautiful, beautiful girl."

Maggie reaches for a condom on the nightstand. Her chest moves close to my face with the stretch, and I capture her breast in my mouth. I suck on her nipple, smiling around the pebbled peak when I hear her moan.

"Aiden."

God, I'm going to miss her saying my name.

"Yeah, sweetheart?"

"We've done everything except me on top. But..." She trails off, eyes hesitant as she rests her hand over my heart.

"Tell me, Maggie, and it's yours."

"I don't want any lists or fantasies. I just want it to be you and me."

If soft and sweet is what she wants, it's what she's going to get.

"Okay." I prop myself up on the pillows. I kiss her and cup her cheek. I stare into her eyes, an infatuated idiot who went and fell for the woman he can't have. "You and me."

I rip open the wrapper and roll the condom down my length. Maggie perches herself above me, waiting, and when I give her a nod to let her know I'm ready, she slowly sinks on me for what might be the final time.

Thank *fuck* we haven't done this with her on top yet. If we had, I'd never let her leave my apartment, because she feels so fucking *good*. Tight, but accommodating, and my cock is right at home. I imagine she's sore, lingering aches from the multiple rounds we've gone, so I let her control the pace. She's in charge, and I'm entirely at her mercy.

She brings herself up my shaft, almost letting my head slip out of her before sliding back down, adjusting to the new angle.

"You feel so good," Maggie says.

A tear catches in her eyes, and I wipe it away with my thumb before it can fall. I kiss her, and I keep kissing her. It's quiet this morning. There aren't any moans or grunts or vulgarities. It truly is just us.

She holds my shoulders, using them for leverage as she rocks her hips. I bite the sensitive part on her chest, right on top of her breast, and I rub her clit in slow, lazy circles.

"I'm going to miss you, sweetheart," I say into the crook of her neck, finally letting the truth spring free. "Take what you need. Use me. It's all yours for a little while longer."

Stay, I want to add.

Don't leave.

But I can't, so I don't. I'm not sure how we'd exist outside these walls. Considering the logistics of a relationship makes my mind hurt. I would never force her into one, either, just because we had a good fuck. So I give in to what I can control. This moment, right here, with a magnificent woman.

Maggie does use me. She moves steadily. A roll here. A slide there. She drags her teeth down the column of my throat, marking me. It's a badge I'll proudly wear for the coming days. I pinch her nipples and palm her breasts, committing the feel to memory. As she gets close, she picks up speed. Her movements turn hurried and frantic. Desperate and needy.

"Are you going to miss my cock, Maggie?" I ask. I give her ass a smack, the skin warm under my palm.

Her back arches and she nods, unbrushed hair spilling over her shoulders. "Yes. You make me feel so good, Aiden." She leans forward, bringing her chest close to mine. "Now fuck me like I deserve."

"With pleasure."

I lift my hips and slam into her. Again and again and again until she cries out, collapsing onto my torso, falling over the edge. I'm mere seconds behind her. I slip my hand into hers and give her palm a squeeze as I fill the latex. No one has ever made me orgasm like this before, and *fuck* I'm going to miss the power she has over me.

"Okay?" Maggie whispers. She brushes a lock of hair away from my forehead.

"Never better, sweetheart. I'm fucking fantastic." She giggles, and I hear her stomach rumble. "C'mon. Let's eat some breakfast."

TWENTY-SIX
MAGGIE

"SO." I cross my legs and watch Aiden. He's bent over the stove, shirtless and flipping a pancake. "Are you doing anything else with your weekend?"

"No. Mae's at her mom's house until tomorrow night. I'm off on Mondays, so tonight will probably be spent on the couch with a glass of whiskey watching some basketball."

"There are worse ways to spend a night."

"And better ones, too." He looks over his shoulder, eyes roaming down my legs. Aiden has seen me completely naked and spread out on his counter, but my body still heats at his gaze. There's still a fire there, the flames yet to extinguish. "What about you?"

"When I checked my phone earlier, I had eighteen messages from Lacey demanding information about last night. Eighteen. So I'll probably spend the night with her." My phone pings again and I roll my eyes, looking down at the screen. "There's another one. Oh. Wait. This is Jeremiah. He texted me a preview of some of the photos. Do you want to see?"

"Sure." He slides breakfast onto two plates for us and takes the stool next to mine. He scoots closer so our knees touch, and he rests his hand on my thigh.

I click the link and wait for the images to download. When they do, I'm flabbergasted. It doesn't look like us. I know it *is* us, but the result is so different from what I imagined. Half the photos are in color, the others are black and white. I click on the first one to enlarge it and giggle. Aiden and I look so awkward sitting on the bench together.

"You look like you want to be anywhere else," he observes. "I didn't realize I'm such horrible company."

"Shut up." I shove his bare shoulder. "I was nervous. I had a hot guy beside me, and I felt like an idiot."

"Oh, please. You did not think I was hot."

"Uh, yeah, I did. My heart skipped a beat when I saw you, and the air left my lungs." Aiden stares at me, his fork halfway to his mouth. "Shit, sorry. That was definitely oversharing."

"No," he says. "It's just... I thought the same thing when I saw you."

"Oh," I whisper. I swallow the lump in my throat, the same one that worked its way up when I was on top of him forty-five minutes ago as I realized it might be my last time touching him. My last time feeling him finish inside me. The last time he'd cup my face and look at me like I'm the most beautiful thing on Earth.

"Keep scrolling. I want to see the others."

We see the snapshot Jeremiah captured of Aiden helping me onto the picnic blanket. The moment where I dropped a piece of cheese and Aiden laughed. Him licking the jam off his hand and my eyes watching his tongue. Us, on the bed, and the way Aiden smiles at me. My hands in his hair and his lips on mine. We look *good* together, like a real couple madly and deeply in love.

"We're hot," I observe, and Aiden chuckles.

"We are. I'm not sure I want my daughter to see these

pictures. She's going to give me shit for days. Fuck, Maggie, you look even hotter the second time I see you in that outfit. How is that possible?"

"I haven't worn lingerie in years. I might need to buy a few more sets."

Aiden goes quiet, and he lets go of my thigh. He takes a bite of his pancake and chews. It takes him a minute to speak again, and when he does, his voice sounds brittle. "Yeah. The green is really nice on you. The red, too."

"As of late, I haven't had a reason to enjoy Valentine's Day. Thank you for showing me that they won't always be terrible."

"Of course." He eats a final bite of pancake and stands, depositing his plate in the sink. "That's what I'm here for."

We spend late morning and early afternoon on the living room couch. We talk about our families and I jot down a list of romance books for Maven to read. The television gets turned on at some point, and we watch a few episodes of a sitcom we both enjoy.

Aiden feeds me lunch, and I clean the dishes from last night and this morning. I spray him with the faucet when he tries to help and he chases me around the kitchen, soap suds on his hands. When he grabs me, he bends me over the barstool and fucks me one last time. I bite the leather to keep from screaming out his name and he rips my shirt off, kissing down my back.

"If you were staying," he whispers as he thrusts into me, "I'd make you lick your mess up off the floor. So needy, aren't you?"

Only for you, I want to say. *No one else has ever made me feel this way.*

After we finish, we trudge back to his room, falling asleep with our limbs wrapped around each other.

"What time is it?" I ask when I wake up. The sun is setting, daylight leaving the world.

"Don't care," he answers through a yawn, pulling me close. "Ten more minutes."

Ten minutes turns to twenty, which turns into two hours as we nap again, his thigh thrown over mine and my cheek against his chest. Soon, it's approaching seven p.m., and we both know what's coming.

"I should..." I trail off and clear my throat.

"Oh. Yeah. Shit, sorry. I didn't mean to keep you so late. That's my fault."

"You didn't. I wanted to stay."

"Right. Yeah. That's good."

It's awkward, and the tension in the room is rising at an alarming rate. This isn't the same chemistry we've had the last twenty-four hours. This feels like two strangers parting ways. It's cold, closed-off. I shimmy off the bed. Aiden grabs a shirt from the floor and yanks it over his head.

"I don't know where half my clothes are."

"Here's your dress."

"Thanks. Have you seen my—"

"Your bra and underwear are near the closet."

"Got it."

"You can change in the bathroom if you want to rinse off before you go."

"That's okay. It's only a few blocks."

Aiden nods and stands, shifting on his feet. "Maggie."

"Yeah?" I put my dress on and look over my shoulder. "Can you zip me up?"

"Sure." He walks toward me and rests his hand on my lower back. He takes his time, kissing the nape of my neck then my throat. "I need to tell you something."

I spin so I can face him. "What? You're dying from an incurable disease and sleeping with a stranger was on your wishlist before you passed?"

He smiles and shakes his head. He cups my cheeks with both hands and looks into my eyes. "I'm going to miss you. A lot."

"You mean you're going to miss my pussy."

"Yes, I am, because it's tight and fucking delicious, but I'm also going to miss *you,* Maggie. Laughing with you. Talking with you. Just being with you. I wanted you to know that before you left."

It doesn't feel like an ultimatum, like he's forcing me to make some life-altering decision. It hurts, though, to hear the words. I'm going to tuck them close and remember them on a particularly lonely day, but I also wish he didn't say them. It reaffirms my suspicions that Aiden and I could have been something.

"I'm going to miss you, too. These have been the best two days of my life."

"Mine too, sweetheart." He kisses my forehead. "You'll take care of yourself, right? You won't let anyone treat you less than the queen you are?"

"I promise."

I'm going to miss you. I'm going to miss you. I'm going to miss you.

"Fuck. I hate hearing that." Aiden takes a step back and runs his hand through his hair. "I don't want to feel like I'm kicking you to the curb, and I don't want some long, drawn-out goodbye. This already sucks. I'm going to go take a shower. You can let yourself out. Deal?"

"Deal," I whisper. I grab his shoulders and kiss him one final time. "Have a good night, Aiden."

"Good night, Maggie."

He glances at me before turning on his heel, hanging his head and closing the bathroom door. I stare at the barrier, knowing I could walk in there if I wanted to. Aiden would let me. This is for the best, though. We got what we wanted out of last night, and that's that.

I sigh and walk to the living room. I grab my bag and slip into my boots. I wrap my coat around my body. I remember the list I wrote last night and hurry to the kitchen, scribbling a quick note down on the lined paper. Then, with an aching heart, I shut the door on Aiden Wood forever.

TWENTY-SEVEN
AIDEN

I KNOW MAGGIE LEFT, but a part of me is optimistic, hopeful she'll there when I get out of the shower. Praying she'll be sitting on the barstool, look over her shoulder, give me a coy smile and say something like "*took you long enough.*"

As I round the corner, I find the apartment, unsurprisingly, empty. It's too quiet in here. I trek to the kitchen and run my hand over the counter, the spot where her ass was a few hours ago. I look at the barstool, her bite marks imprinted in the leather. Her note is still out and I pick it up. My eyes spot two new sentences at the bottom of the paper.

I'll think of you whenever I try one of these again. Thank you, Aiden.

The worst part isn't imagining her with another man. It's the little heart she added, above the i in my name.

I want to rip the paper to shreds.

I pull my phone out and dial Shawn's number. It rings twice before he answers.

"How was—"

"I need a drink." I interrupt him before he can ask. "Are you free?"

"Of course. Practice ended a bit ago. You want me to come over?"

"No. I need to get out of here."

"Come to my place. I have food."

"And alcohol?"

"Lots of alcohol."

"I'll be there soon."

I decide to walk. The air is cold, numbing my face as I make the four-block trek to his penthouse in a luxury condo building a few streets up. By the time I'm riding the elevator to the top floor, my hands are red and my eyes are watering.

"You look like shit," Shawn says when he opens the door.

"I feel like shit." I walk into his foyer and hang my jacket on his coat rack. A crystal glass gets thrust into my hand, amber liquid sloshing around.

"Bourbon. Thought it might help."

I finish it in one swallow. "Got any more?"

Thirty minutes later, I'm feeling the effects of limited food and copious amounts of alcohol. My vision is blurry and my limbs are heavy. I'm sprawled out across Shawn's leather couch, arm draped over my head.

"Spill, Aiden."

"Maggie is incredible. I'm an idiot. What else do you want to know?"

"So you had a good night together?"

I groan as I sit up. "We did, and it wasn't just because of the sex. Which was amazing, by the way. Everything with her was awesome. Talking with her. Kissing her. Just sitting in silence. I don't know. I know I've been out of the game for years, but it never felt like that with Katie."

Shawn whistles. "Okay. She left, and you didn't chase after her?"

"No, because I'm a moron. I should have. I told her I'd miss her, and she said she would miss me, too. But then I got out of my shower and she wasn't there."

"Because you didn't ask her to stay."

"She didn't tell me she wanted to stay either."

"Seriously?" Shawn groans. "Dude, c'mon. Listen to me. I've had a lot of one-night stands."

"Define a lot."

"Twenty?"

"Jesus Christ. I'm going to die without ever having sex again, aren't I? This one time was too good to be true."

"Shut up. Do you know how my one-night stands usually go? The woman comes to my place, or I go there. We spend a couple hours together. The second the sun rises, either I leave, or I escort her out. There's no personal shit. No making breakfast or lunch. I don't learn her middle name or what her favorite color is. It's sex. That's it. What you did is not just sex."

"So I fucked up royally, because that's all it's supposed to be."

"Yeah, because you put a limit on it. You clearly felt a connection with her, more than you have with any other woman who has tried to get your attention in the last five years. And the best part is she felt a connection, too. It's why she stayed so long, Aiden. It's not hard to bang one time then leave."

"So what the hell do I do?"

"I think you have to wait."

"Wait for what?"

"I don't know. A sign from the universe."

"You want me to put my future in the hands of the universe," I draw out. "Great, I'll be waiting for years."

"Yesterday you didn't want a relationship and today you do? What changed?"

"Her. Maybe I'm drunk on Maggie, but it would be so easy with her. Every conversation we had was easy, Shawn. The second she walked out, I realized how badly I wanted her back. And not because I wanted to fuck her. Because I wanted to hold her through the night and hear what else she had to say."

"You've got it bad."

"No shit." I sigh and rub my temples. "This hurts to say, but I think I'm going to wait a little bit. Not because I don't miss her. I miss her already. An indescribable amount. But because I want to be completely sure about this, and I want her to be sure, too. I want her to miss me. To go through these same emotions as me, wondering if I'm thinking about her. Maybe in a couple weeks I'll reach out. We can revisit things with fresh, clear minds. I don't want her to make a lust-driven decision."

"That's a good plan. She might crack first. The sex was that good?"

"She rocked my world."

"Okay. I don't need all the details, but give me *something*."

"I made her crawl to me and she did it willingly. Ate her out on the counter, too."

"Holy fuck. You lucky bastard."

"And she's smart as hell. Literally the perfect woman. I'm so fucked."

"I'm happy for you, man. At the very least, if things don't pan out with Maggie, you got your groove back. You can bag any woman you want."

"I don't want any woman," I say. "I want her."

"Then wait," Shawn says. He pushes my legs off the couch cushion and sits next to me. "One day soon, you'll know when it's time to reach out."

"Is the universe going to wave a big sign my way so I know what to do and when?"

"Maybe. Maybe it'll be more subtle. But when it's time, you'll know."

"God, what would I even say? 'Hey, I know we had one night together, but I think I could spend the rest of my life with you?' That's not fucking creepy at all."

"Will you relax?" Shawn chuckles. "You weren't even this worked up when you asked Katie to marry you."

"Yeah, because Katie was a sure thing. I knew she was going to say yes. Maggie? I have no clue if I'll ever see her again. And if I do, I don't know if she'll feel the same way I do about her."

"So you're scared."

"I'm fucking terrified."

"It sounds like she's your soulmate."

"Soulmates are a load of shit."

"Are they?" Shawn arches his eyebrow. "You've never come over to my place and downed half a bottle of bourbon to talk about a woman before. And then suddenly you meet someone at a photo shoot you weren't going to do, have the best night of your life, then miss her when she's gone? If that's not a soulmate, I don't know what is, man."

I grunt and ignore him. I curl onto my side and close my eyes, hoping the alcohol is enough not to dream about Maggie and her pretty hair and wonderful smile. It's been three hours since she left, and I'm already going out of my mind.

I don't stand a fucking chance at surviving the coming weeks.

What the hell kind of sign am I waiting for?

TWENTY-EIGHT
MAGGIE

THE WEATHER TURNS MILD. March arrives and staves off the blistering cold air. The sun thaws the snow left behind from a big storm, lingering in the sky a little longer every day. It's not quite spring when tulips bloom and all you need is a light jacket, but it's a reprieve from the Arctic blast we experienced over the last few weeks.

The last few weeks where I've been restless, doing everything in my power to avoid thinking about Aiden. Whenever the vision of him manifests—the smile he wears early in the morning while doling out a plate of pancakes, the tenderness in his eyes as he tells me I'm beautiful, the sturdiness of his palm under my body, whispering that I'm safe and he's got me—I throw myself into other parts of my life.

I go to the hospital, offering to work overtime two, three times a week to keep my mind occupied. I pick up a book and disappear into a fantasy world, finding comfort and solace in far-off lands with swashbuckling heroes. And, as of late, I lace up my new sneakers and power walk.

Lacey and I are moving at a brisk pace down the bike path running parallel to the Potomac. The monuments on our right gleam under the light of high noon, reflections of yellow catching in the gentle river waves. A jogger passes us with a wave, her enthusiastic vigor for exercise causing Lacey and I to exchange a look and dissolve into giggles.

We stop for a breather, pulling off to the side and taking a seat on a cluster of rocks. The sharp edges scrape against the back of my thighs as I get comfortable, staring out across the water. Aiden's out there, somewhere, amongst the buildings and trees and the thousands of other residents of our metropolis. Walking down the street. Saving children. Spending time with his daughter. Living life, undeterred by our expeditious parting.

It pains me to reminisce, to ruminate on the mess of his hair when he gets out of the shower and the spare pillows he keeps in his closet. I kick a pebble and watch it career down the steep slope into the waiting pool of water below.

"I can't stop thinking about him," I admit through a rush of words, breaking the silence. "I haven't since I left his apartment."

It's the first time I've spoken the truth out loud and acknowledged the validity of feelings I've kept locked inside. When I told Lacey details about my night with Aiden, I talked about the physical components; how hot it was. The positions we tried. The new things I discovered I liked. I never once mentioned the deeper feelings that wove their way through the twenty-four hours, and the lingering ache in my heart in all the time that has passed.

I'm glad they're out and I'm sharing the secret with the world. It's a burden I no longer have to carry alone.

"I know you haven't," Lacey says. She doesn't seem fazed by the admission, and I wonder how obvious I've been with my sulking. "Why don't you track him down?"

"Why can't he track me down?" I argue. "He has my number, too."

"You're running." She pins me with a pointed look, and I

avert my eyes. I focus on the patch of weeds growing at the base of a nearby tree.

"I'm not running. He opened the door for me."

"But did he push you out?"

I'm unable to formulate a response. *No*, I think, *he didn't*. He practically offered to keep me there forever, if I wanted. And, *god*, I wanted to say yes. In hindsight, if I had known I would be shrouded in loneliness since I left, I would've stayed. I would have spent another night with him, then another, and another, piling up until four years had passed in the blink of an eye.

"Maybe it's supposed to be this way. Maybe the universe gave him to me as an offering, so I could realize I can be with someone again. Aiden said he doesn't want a relationship, and I doubt he's sitting around thinking about me."

"God, I want to shake you. Mags, you're the smartest person I've ever met. Did it ever occur to you that maybe he was telling you what you wanted to hear? He said the things that would make you agree, even if he didn't care to go along with them himself?"

I pause and consider this angle. "If that's the case, wouldn't he have reached out to me by now?"

"No, because that's not what you want. Allegedly."

"So he's a liar."

"He's a man who listens," Lacey corrects me. "We read books all the time about men who run after women they love, but we also read about men who let the woman dictate how the story ends. Wouldn't you rather hold the power to write your own conclusion, however you see fit, instead of having pressure from someone else to decide on their behalf?"

She's right.

I want to be wanted, but I don't want to be chased. I'm sure plenty of women do; they need the groveling and the grand gesture, the pining and running across the city to have the man's feelings proved to them. It might make me an anomaly, but I have to decide on my own, unswayed by opinions of those around me. If Aiden had reached out, if he had tracked me down, I might have panicked.

The longer I think about it, though, with each passing day, the answer becomes more clear. I want him. I want him more than I've ever wanted anyone in my entire life. I want him at night, his body hovering over mine as he presses a kiss to my chest. In the morning, sweatpants hanging off his hips and a spatula in his hands. I want to meet his daughter and his friends. I want every part of him.

There's always the chance, the terrifying possibility he doesn't feel the same way. In the back of my mind, I can't help but wonder *why* he hasn't attempted to track me down. He has my number. Finding me would be easy.

Does he know me better than I think he does? Am I that easy to read?

A breeze filters through the air and blows my hair into my face. I tuck a piece behind my ear and lift my chin. My gaze wanders across the water, over to the buildings again. I rub my neck over the spot of the hickey that sat there, the phantom touch of Aiden's lips pressing into my bare skin. I wonder how long the sensation will follow me, taunting me through various parts of my day.

When I put my hair into a bun for work, I imagine him yanking on my scalp so my mouth falls open. In the shower, as I wash my legs, I remember him kneeling in front of me, tongue running up my inner thigh, a wicked glint in his eyes. On my bed as I try to fall asleep, his sturdy arms and the softness of his chest behind me are absent, nowhere to be found.

"Do you think I'm harboring these feelings because it's the first time I've been with a man since my divorce? Maybe I'm making a mountain out of a molehill. Maybe he has healing powers, and I'm cured from my plague of no orgasms and being underappreciated."

"There's an easy way to test that theory," Lacey says. "Sleep with someone else."

A deep frown takes root on my lips. I don't want to sleep with anyone else. I don't want anyone else looking at me like I'm someone to worship. I don't want someone else brushing my sweat-soaked hair off my forehead, a kiss pressed into the perspiration.

"I don't think I can."

"Well." Lacey grins. "There's your answer."

"We got invited to do an interview with *Wake Up, America* next week, talking about the photo shoot since it's gone viral. Jeremiah will be there. I imagine Aiden will go, too, so maybe it'll be our chance to reconnect." I blow out a breath and pull my jacket tight around my body. It's growing colder, the sun covered by a patch of clouds. "I can wait a few days. I deserve this happiness again. I've spent years searching for it, and I finally found it. Aiden makes me happy."

"You deserve it and more." Lacey reaches over and squeezes my hand.

I squeeze her back, decision made. I'm going to find Aiden Wood and get a second chance at this whole happily ever after thing. Maybe this time, it will stick.

TWENTY-NINE
MAGGIE

AIDEN ISN'T HERE.

I expected him to be. I expected to see him on the train from D.C. to New York. I expected to find him in the elevator, the two of us having an awkward run-in as the doors closed and I tried to hold them open. I expected him to be next to me on the couch, getting a microphone hooked onto the collar of his shirt.

But he isn't.

The thought plagues me as an assistant on *Wake Up, America* fixes rogue pieces of my hair, sweeping the loose strands away from my eyes. Across from me, Deborah, the host of the show, studies her cue cards. Her lips move as she silently practices the interview questions.

Jeremiah plops down next to me on the couch. He takes my hand. "Are you doing okay?"

"Yeah." My eyes drop to the space on my other side, and I sigh. "I just thought—"

"So did I."

"It's fine. Really. No big deal. It's just a couple of questions, and we can forget the shoot ever happened."

"Do you want to forget the shoot ever happened?" Jeremiah asks.

"No. I want Aiden to be here and I want him to be the one holding my hand, not you. Sorry. You know I love you."

"But I can't dick you down like he can. I get it. I'm allowed to be replaced."

I giggle. "Stop. You're going to make me cry and I think the makeup lady already wants to kill me for all the bags under my eyes she had to cover up."

"You look as beautiful as always to me." Jeremiah plants a kiss on my cheek.

"Thanks, Jer."

"We're live in ten," someone calls out. Music begins to play and the set goes silent. My spine stiffens with anticipation and I sit up as straight as I can, folding my ankles over themselves.

"Welcome back, folks," Deborah says, staring into the camera. "I'm joined now by Maggie Houston and Jeremiah Porter, who recently went viral with their strangers' photo shoot. You might have seen the pictures floating around social media—how could you not? The images are everywhere, and rightfully so. Jeremiah, let's start with you. Working with two people who don't know each other. They aren't models. It's like picking someone off a street. Why?"

"Deborah, thank you so much for having us this morning," Jeremiah starts. "The trend gained popularity a few years back, and there's something so fascinating to me about watching a story unfold from behind the lens. I didn't give any direction; I let Maggie and Aiden be who they are, and that's where the chemistry happened. They were so dynamic, and easier to photograph than a lot of the professionals I've worked with, because they connected so well."

"Do you think we could expect more of these shoots to pop up in the future?"

"I certainly hope so," he says. "I wanted to incorporate humans you would see walking down the street or on the Metro. The industry is changing; more body types are being showcased in ads and on the runway. Our shoot proves we as photographers could also afford to get away from some of the rigidity associated with formal photo shoots, and let the models do what feels right in the moment."

"Beautifully said." Deborah turns to me. "Now, Maggie, this was out of your element, yes? Clearly you're not a model."

"Professionals don't pose with their mouth half open?" I joke, taking the backhanded comment in stride. "I'm a neurosurgeon, actually, and I usually hate being in front of a camera."

"Our senior prom photos are so bad," Jeremiah adds.

"Jer is my best friend, and I could hear how passionate he was when talking about the idea. I agreed to do the shoot, and once some of the initial tension wore off, I had a great time."

"Has there been any backlash? Any critique that, as a doctor, you shouldn't be posing in your underwear? What kind of message do you think that sends?"

Jeremiah stiffens beside me, and my smile falls. "Women, and men, should be allowed to express themselves creatively through nonprofessional outlets. Maybe that's a tattoo, or a new hair color. Or, in this case, photography. There are pictures on my social media of me at a beach in less clothing than what I had on at the shoot. Those are acceptable. And somehow this isn't? What one does in their free time doesn't impact their reliability in their career. Most of the feedback has been positive, and I love that people can see that all bodies should be celebrated on camera."

"Wonderful. Now for the elephant in the room. Everyone wants to know about you and Aiden. Did you really not know each other before the shoot?"

"No. We met that day."

"And a connection formed. Have you seen each other since?"

My heart hammers so loudly in my chest, I'd be surprised if the camera didn't pick up the erratic beat. "No," I answer. "We haven't."

"Is a reconciliation something you'd be open to?" Deborah presses. I feel like I'm on a shitty dating show and my baggage is being carried across the stage for all to see.

"Aiden and I knew the parameters of the shoot going in, and we've stuck to that. He's a great man, and a loving father. I enjoyed our time together, and I hope he's doing well."

"If you could say anything to him, what would it be?"

I miss you. I think about you day and night. Do you think about me?

"I would ask when the appointment for his tattoo removal is."

It's a pathetic joke, an easy way out from this hell I've been thrust into. I don't want to relive our intimate moments on national television without him by my side. It's wrong, an attention I don't deserve.

"Oh, you are a hoot, aren't you? We're going to take a quick commercial break. When we come back, we'll have Deals with Demi. See you soon," Deborah says. The camera clicks off, and she turns to me with a grin. "He must have been a good fuck. Why else would you be so elusive? I can see it. He's got the whole dad bod thing going. I don't find it attractive, but I'm glad some women do."

My cheeks burn and rage boils in me. "Pardon?"

Deborah waves her hand and stands. "Yeah. It's always the ones you don't expect to be good who really blow your mind, huh?"

I stand too. "Who cares what his body looks like? Aiden is a great guy. Sorry you're a vapid woman who is shallow enough to only date a guy because of his physical attributes. And by the way, if I wanted to say something to him publicly, I wouldn't do it on your show. So much for empowering women, huh? Thanks for slut-shaming me on national television."

I storm off set, ripping the microphone from my shirt. Jeremiah follows behind me after adding a few choice words to the host as well. "Mags," he says, catching up to me. "Are you okay?"

"No, I'm not okay. I miss him, Jeremiah. A whole fucking lot."

"I know, sweetie." He gives me a hug, and I'm surprised when I start to cry.

"I thought he would be here today. I thought he would send me a message. But every day that goes by and he doesn't, I think he's forgotten me when I can't get him out of my damn head."

"I don't think he's forgotten about you, Mags. I think he's just scared."

"Yeah, well, I'm scared too."

"I hate seeing you like this. You weren't even this bent out of shape after your divorce."

"Do you think it makes me look pathetic if I reach out?"

"No," Jeremiah says. "It means you haven't given up. It means you have hope."

"Hope," I repeat. I smile at the word. "Sometimes, that's half the battle."

THIRTY

AIDEN

I COULD HAVE LOVED HER.

It's a forlorn realization, a discovery made far too late. With time, though, it would have happened. Easily. I would have fallen hopelessly and irrevocably in love with Maggie Houston, because she's a woman you don't let out of your sight.

But I did, like a moron. I didn't bother to fight or make an argument about why she should stay. It's not what she wanted, and, more than anything, I want to give her exactly what she wants. Even if it doesn't include me.

I can still feel her legs around my waist. Her skin, soft and smooth, under the palm of my hands as a bead of sweat rolls down her cheek. I can hear the echo of her moans against the four corners of my room and the smell of her hair—like springtime flowers—lingers on my pillowcase.

I flip onto my side and stare at the empty space she once occupied. A lifetime has passed, while at the same time, no time has passed at all. The bed is colder without her here. The room, darker, a light extinguished and a flame snuffed out.

Fuck, I miss her.

My chest aches, a physical ailment plaguing me the longer

my eyes fixate on the wrinkled cotton. I run my palm across the sheets and heave a sigh. It makes no sense, an unexplainable phenomenon as to how she worked herself into my life so quickly without a substantial amount of time.

Making a snap decision, half-drunk and feeling a little stupid after watching her interview earlier in the afternoon during a quick break at work, I grab my phone off the nightstand and find Maggie's contact info. We exchanged numbers before leaving the photo shoot, in case either of us changed our minds about meeting up. There are no messages there, not yet. Before I can think twice or talk myself off the ledge I've climbed, my fingers fly across the screen, typing the first communication.

Aiden: Hate to disappoint—no tattoo removal for me.

I hit send before I can regret the pathetic opening line. There's no merit to it, but, at the very least, I hope it makes her laugh.

I don't have to wait long for a response. It takes less than two minutes for my phone to ding.

Maggie: Millions would mourn the loss.

Then, in quick succession,

Maggie: You saw the interview, I take it?

Aiden: Yeah, I did. You were great. That host sucked.

Maggie: She was the worst. I thought you would be there.

Maggie: I was disappointed when you weren't.

The air leaves my lungs and I pause, not knowing the correct way to answer.

Aiden: You looked beautiful.

Maggie: Thank you.

Aiden: I wanted to be there, but Maven had a swim meet. I'm sorry you had to go through that alone.

Maggie: It's okay. Jeremiah and I gave her an earful.

Aiden: Atta girl. I would have done the same.

It's past midnight, and I'm not sure what else to say. We

should both be asleep, because nothing good will come from this. It doesn't show her typing, either, the natural conclusion of a stilted conversation I never should have initiated. I'm about to click my phone closed for good and delete the thread, when it buzzes again.

Maggie: I miss you.

The air leaves my lungs. I read the three words a hundred times, making sure they're actually there. When they stare back at me, eight letters causing my heart to clench and my palms to sweat, I decide to say *fuck it*, and let her know she's on my mind.

Aiden: I miss you too, sweetheart.

Maggie: How was your day? How was Maven's swim meet?

I smile, imagining her in bed and thinking about me.

Aiden: She won. The kid is like a fish when it comes to water.

Maggie: That's awesome. I bet you're so proud.

Aiden: I have a T-shirt with her face on it and everything. She hates it.

Maggie: She might say that, but deep down, I bet you being there means more to her than anything else in the world.

Aiden: I think so, too.

Maggie: I did something bad, Aiden.

Aiden: You did?

Maggie: I lied on national television.

Aiden: Oh? Are you the one with the incurable disease?

Maggie: That made me smile.

Aiden: Then I'm doing my job.

Maggie: If I could say one thing to you, it wouldn't have been about your tattoo.

Aiden: Now I'm intrigued. You better not shit on my jarred spaghetti sauce. You almost licked that bowl clean.

I wait for her to answer. Three dots show she's typing, then disappear. I'm patient, knowing it's taking her a minute to convince herself what she wants to say is important. Then, my phone buzzes again.

Maggie: Would it be okay if I called?

Aiden: Is saying fuck yes too aggressive?

I grin when I see the incoming call.

"Hey, sweetheart," I answer.

"You're not supposed to be calling me that," she responds. There's no malice in her tone, and I hear the hint of a smile.

"What's up?"

"I can't sleep. Some guy keeps texting me."

"He sounds horrible."

"He's not too bad."

I adjust my position on the bed, flipping to my back and staring at the ceiling. *God,* it's good to hear her voice. "So the interview sucked, huh?"

"I hate being in front of cameras. The woman said some nasty things to me after the segment, too. It would have been a lot better with you there."

"I'm sorry I didn't give you a heads up. I didn't know if you'd want me there in the first place, or if you'd miss me when I didn't show up."

"I missed you."

"So. What would you have said to me?"

Maggie takes a deep breath. "I would have said that I wish I didn't walk out of your apartment. I wish I stayed, and I wish I did a better job of conveying that to you. I hate the miscommunication trope in books, and I—"

"What the hell is the miscommunication trope?"

"It's when the couple doesn't communicate properly and you want to bash their heads in for being so stupid."

"I thought we did a good job of communicating." I rub my jaw. "Hang on. Want to FaceTime?"

"I'm in bed without any clothes on."

I've never initiated a FaceTime so quickly in my life. Maggie pops up on my screen, the glow of her phone reflecting on her face. "Sorry. You can't tell me you're naked and not expect me to call."

She laughs and tucks her arm under her cheek, smiling at me. She's pixelated, a little fuzzy, but she's *there*. "I guess I kind of walked into that one," she agrees.

"So, miscommunication. You wish you didn't leave, but you did. Why?"

"I don't know." Maggie sighs, and the sheet around her chest slips an inch. "We both said we didn't want a relationship, and I was afraid what I was feeling was a result of any sort of attention from a man, not just from you."

"What are your thoughts now?"

"It's you I miss. It's you I wanted to stay for."

"I would have let you. The second you left I wanted to bust into the hall and chase you down. I didn't, though, because I didn't think it was what you wanted." I pause and shake my head. "Fuck, you're right. Miscommunication is the fucking worst."

"Told you."

"What do you want now?"

"Now? Now I want to see you again."

"Maggie Houston. Are you propositioning me again?"

"Propositioning you would be if I brought my phone between my legs and let you see how wet I am."

I groan and bury my face in my pillow. "You fucking menace. Stop before I pay for an Uber so you get your ass over here tonight."

"You could come over here." It's a timid suggestion, one I know she's nervous to ask. She bites her lip and her eyes dart away.

"Look at me, sweetheart." Her gaze moves back up to the screen. "Trust me. If my daughter wasn't down the hall, I'd be at your front door already."

"In that case... Do you want to get dinner sometime this week? I'm sure you're busy and so am I, but—"

"Say the day, Maggie, and I'll be there, even if it means rearranging my whole schedule."

"Thursday night? That's only three days away."

I smile at her, exhaustion and glee hitting me like a tidal wave. "I'm going to have to buy you a coffee after, to honor my promise to my meddling daughter, but yeah. Thursday. It's a date, sweetheart."

THIRTY-ONE

AIDEN

I AM EXHAUSTED.

Maggie and I stayed up and talked for three hours, filling each other in on everything in our lives from the past few weeks we've been apart. When we finally said goodbye after she fell asleep mid-sentence, it was nearing four a.m. My alarm went off just past six, and I've never hated a sound so much in my life.

I yawn and rub my temples to rid the headache forming. A quick check of my schedule tells me I'm free for the next hour, and I'm in desperate need of some caffeine to keep me awake. Instead of heading for the break room pot of coffee that's been sitting out for god knows how long, I decide to go to the cafeteria downstairs, needing a change of scenery and to stretch my legs.

This is why I go to bed early. I'm a zombie incapable of functioning correctly the next day after a night stretching past ten p.m.

Through another yawn, I step into the elevator, finding a spot tucked away in the corner. Two doctors file in behind me and nod hello. After the greeting, they lean into each other to whisper conspiratorially. There's been an uptick in attention on me since the photo shoot. I knew that would happen. It was inevitable when the photos went viral, but it's awkward to know you're being talked about by your peers, and not some stranger on the internet.

Ignoring the conversation unfolding beside me, I tap my foot to the beat of the jazz music crooning softly over the speakers. It's a soothing compilation, one that quiets my brain for the first time in days.

The doors open and I let the other occupants exit before I make my way down the hall. My phone buzzes in my pocket as I push inside the crowded cafeteria. Nurses and patients' families mill about, in search of sustenance.

When I pull out the device, I see Maven's name on the screen. I'm about to answer her message when a shoulder bumps into mine. I'm knocked to the side and my phone tumbles to the ground.

"Shit," a voice says. "I'm so sorry."

I know that voice.

That voice whispered in my ear about how *good* I made her feel. How *close* she was to finishing. How *badly* she needed me. That voice said goodnight to me over FaceTime last night, an exhausted smile on her lips and my name a breathy song. I close my eyes and take a deep breath.

I must be imagining it. Manifesting what I *want* to see or hear. I'll wait five seconds, then I'll look.

I count slowly, staving off the inevitable disappointment that's going to come when I find out who just ran into me. It's probably someone doing their residency, a frazzled kid who hasn't slept in days. It *can't* be who I want it to be.

One. Two. Three. Four. Five.

My eyes blink open, and I raise my chin. There, standing three feet away, coffee down the front of her blue scrubs and her hair in a ponytail, is Maggie.

She's staring at me, jaw slack and eyes wide. Her limbs seem to have become frozen because she's unmoving, a statue amid people meandering around us.

"Aiden?" she whispers.

"Maggie? What... what are you doing here?"

"I work here."

"You work *here?*" I ask. "At Uptown Medical?"

"Yes."

"You're a neurosurgeon on the eighth floor?"

Maggie nods once. "And you... you also work here?"

"I'm on the second floor."

Her hand flies to her mouth. "Pediatric oncology. Oh, my god. Are you serious?"

"I just started my fourteenth year."

"I can't... this is..." Her head shakes and her lip quivers. "Sorry. I knew I would see you in a couple of days, but it's entirely different to run into you in a place where we both— holy shit. We work in the same building. I'm kind of freaking out."

"Is it a good-freak out, or a bad-freak out?" I ask.

"A good-freak out," Maggie says. "I meant what I said the other night. I've missed you an unthinkable amount. More than anyone should after just a few hours with someone, but it's the truth."

We talked for hours last night, but I didn't have the chance to tell her how much I wanted to be with her. I didn't admit to her she's all I've thought about, every waking hour spent wondering if she was okay, if she was happy.

God damn Shawn and his sign from the universe.

How else do you explain the woman I'm crazy about running into me in the cafeteria at the place where we both work? Divine intervention? Fate? Sheer dumb luck?

Whatever it is, I'm grabbing hold. I'm done fucking waiting because she's looking at me, waiting to hear what I have to say, and there isn't enough time left in my lifetime to tell her everything.

"God, Maggie," I finally get out. My shirt is tight on my skin. My face is warm. I want to pull her into a hug and never let go. "You look incredible. I've missed you, sweetheart. So fucking much. More than a stupid text message or FaceTime call could ever convey."

"You really did?" Her whispered question is hesitant, a ghost of a confession and a painful wait to hear what else I might have to say.

"Every single day was miserable. I didn't know if I was even allowed to miss you, or to feel some emotion beyond temporary attraction. Then I realized how empty my apartment is without you in it. How dull my life is without your laughter. It might have been only one night, but I would have missed you for eternity."

Tears leak from her eyes, and she bats them away with the back of her hand. She closes the distance between us, arms wrapping around my neck and pulling me close. I kiss her chin, her cheek, her forehead. I kiss any inch of her skin I can find, a million of them to make up for the time we've spent apart.

"I was a fool to let you go," I whisper into the crook of her neck. My palms smooth down her back, coming to rest on her waist. I don't think I'll get over how *right* she fits in my arms. Like a piece of myself—my soul—was missing until she pressed herself against me. And now I'm whole.

"We were six floors apart this entire time. We might not have found each other if not for the photo shoot." Maggie buries her face into the collar of my shirt, tears staining my tie. I hold her tighter, experiencing the same rush of sadness and regret, a near suffocating feeling. "I hate that, Aiden."

"No," I say fiercely. "I would have always found you, sweetheart, even if it took me years of searching every goddamn hospital. I would have torn the world apart to learn your name and find your smile. And when I did, I would have known right away you were the one, just like I did the second I walked into that warehouse. My life was boring until I met you. Now all I see are colors, and light, and your beautiful, perfect face. I want you, Maggie Houston, however you'll have me, for the rest of my life."

The sound of clattering trays, the smell of pizza and French fries, the sight of a hundred people watching us embrace in the middle of a crowded room fade away, until it's only her and I. Time stops, exactly how it did when we shook hands for the first time, when I kissed her for the first time, when I buried myself in her for the first time. I'm waiting to hear if she feels the same way I do. Everything hinges on this next moment.

"I want you too, Aiden Wood," she says. Her words ring in my ears. Balloons drop from the ceiling. Trumpets play and choirs sing. Confetti litters the floor. In my mind, every obnoxious display of celebration is exploding like fireworks sparkling in the night sky. "I want your cooking. Your tattoo. The love you have for your daughter. In every capacity, every minute of every day."

"Well, it sounds like I have a very important question to ask, then."

"What's that?"

"Maggie Houston," I say in the shell of her ear. She giggles, and the sound buoys me, the ebb and flow of life starting anew. "Fuck dinner. I'm not going another minute without you in my life. I don't care if it's cheesy or stupid or some happily ever after from your romance novels. Will you do me the greatest honor and get a cup of shitty cafeteria coffee with me?"

"Yeah," she says, a constellation of stars dazzling in her eyes and my heart in her hands, a future yet to come. "I'd love to."

ACKNOWLEDGMENTS

I hope you enjoyed this fun, on a whim novella I wrote. The idea came to me randomly one day, and I couldn't stop thinking about Maggie and Aiden. I toyed with the idea of making it a longer novel, but this length felt adequate for their story. I hope you agree!

Thank you for reading! I appreciate you taking the time to read my words. I'm always grateful people to continue to give me a chance to show my development as a writer. I hope to keep getting better. This is my spiciest book yet, with less plot and more fun, but I had a good time writing something a little less heavy!

Bonnie, Skyler, Katie, Katelin, Haley, Amanda, Kristen and Dani: Thank you for being my beta readers. I appreciate your quick and thorough feedback. This book wouldn't be possible without you.

Britt: Thank you for putting up with me and my chaotic timelines. You're an angel.

Sam: I'm not sure there will come a day where I don't cry at a cover you design. You're a creative genius, and I can't wait to keep working with you.

Bookstagram and BookTok: Thanks for continuing to support indie authors and make our dreams come true. Every comment, every message, every share means the world to us. You all are incredible.

My family: Love you all. Sorry for typing this on our cruise, Courtney, and keeping you awake.

And finally, Mikey and Riley: I know we don't celebrate Valentine's Day, but I'm the luckiest girl to have you guys. I wouldn't want to go through my DINK life with anyone else. The jetski is coming. I promise. I love you.

ABOUT THE AUTHOR

Chelsea Curto splits her time between Winter Park, Florida and Boston, Massachusetts, where she's based as a flight attendant. When she's not busy writing, she loves to read, travel, go to theme parks, run, eat tacos, hang out with friends and pet dogs. Come say hi on social media!

ALSO BY CHELSEA CURTO

First series (stand-alone interconnected books)

An Unexpected Paradise

The Companion Project

Park Cove Series (stand-alone interconnected books)

Booked for the Holidays

———

Stay tuned for more books publishing soon!

Lacey and Shawn's story will drop in December 2023!

Made in the USA
Monee, IL
13 April 2024

56913398R00105